Wings
of
Olympus

Wings of Olympus

BY

KALLIE GEORGE

HARPER

An Imprint of HarperCollinsPublishers

Wings of Olympus

www.harpercollinschildrens.com
Library of Congress Control Number: 2018962275
ISBN 978-0-06-274152-3
Typography by Joe Merkel
19 20 21 22 23 CG/LSCH 10 9 8 7 6 5 4 3 2 1
❖
First Edition

To Luke, who met me when this story was first taking flight.
And to Ori, whose story is just beginning
—K.G.

Long ago, on the southern slopes of mighty Mount Olympus, in a house with a roof made of sky, lived the three Fates. Although they were always busy spinning, measuring, and snipping the threads of mortal lives, their work gave them plenty of time to talk. They liked arguing best.

"Might!" snapped Atropos, brandishing her shears. "Might is greater than love. The thicker the thread the better."

"Love!" insisted Lachesis, tapping her measuring rod. "Love is greater than might! Two threads are better than one!"

"Bother," muttered Clotho, pulling back her spindle. The thread she'd been spinning had snapped.

Rain was falling now, and Atropos and Lachesis were too busy arguing about who was getting wetter to notice the snapped thread. Before they did, before Clotho could change her mind, she knotted the thread back together. She hated when threads snapped before they were snipped.

Of course, she wasn't supposed to fix threads that broke. She wasn't supposed to meddle. But where was the fun in that?

She was a Fate, after all.

One

There was magic in the storm. Pippa's skin tingled. Rain beat down on the tile roof of the stables like the hooves of a hundred horses, and, through the window, she watched lightning bolts flash in the distance. Zeus, king of Mount Olympus, god of the sky, was saying something. But what?

The horse in the stall behind her, an old mare, pawed anxiously at the ground, interrupting Pippa's thoughts. The groom, Alcaeus, who was in charge of the horses, would likely appear any moment to tend to the mare, and the stables still weren't clean.

Pippa had been working there for over a year. The South Wall Stables, on the outskirts of Athens, were the largest she'd known, housing the horses of traveling merchants, as well as a few for the master of the house and his son.

I'd better get back to work, Pippa thought, but was interrupted again, this time by another flash. Not of lightning, but something else. A giant wing, feathery and silver, dipped from beneath the clouds like a sideways sail—there one moment and gone the next.

Pippa gasped.

Only one creature had a wing that size—a winged horse.

She couldn't help herself. She rushed out of the stables, into the storm, eager to get another look. Instantly she was drenched, but she barely noticed. All of her attention was focused upward on the clouds, hoping for another glimpse.

Could it be? Had she seen Nikomedes, Zeus's steed? Zeus had had many horses since Pegasus retired long ago to the skies as a constellation, and Pippa tried her best to keep track of them. She had heard tales of Nikomedes's silver wings and golden hooves, though of course she'd never seen him before now. No one had, as far as she knew.

Pippa raced on. Along the pathway that ran through the master's property, the *oikos*, and out onto the cobblestone road that wound its way toward the *agora*, the marketplace, the heart of Athens.

Although the road usually bore merchants and carts, laborers and messengers (and even the rare bandit), now it was empty. Everyone had taken shelter.

Everyone except Pippa. The coarse cloth of her tunic clung to her skin, and her bare legs and feet were muddy. But on she went—past the mud-bricked inn that housed travelers, and the olive trees soaking up the rain—chasing the retreating clouds . . . until her foot struck a stone and she tumbled forward, landing in a puddle with a splash.

She rolled out of the puddle and sat, hugging her legs to her chest. One knee was scraped, and both were covered in muck. Her big toe, which she'd stubbed, throbbed. *What was I thinking!* She was just a foundling, without parents or a home. Foundlings didn't glimpse the steeds of the gods. That was for the likes of the all-seeing Oracle and other priests and priestesses and . . .

. . . Song-stitchers? A staff appeared in front of Pippa's face. Covered in intricate carvings, it was the staff of a *rhapsode*—a song-stitcher, reciter of myths and teller of tales. Pippa knew, for she had spent her earliest years in the care of one, an old woman named Zosime. Zosime had found her when she was a baby and cared for her until she was old enough to look out for herself.

But whereas Zosime had been well-kept, this song-stitcher was the opposite. Her face was thin, her weathered skin stretched over bone, and her eyes were sunken and dark, like the pits of two olives. She wore a long woolen *himation*, which wound across her hunched shoulders and up over her head like a hood, shielding her from the rain. Across her back was slung a lyre, some of its strings broken and bobbing in the wind like unruly strands of hair. Even her staff was chipped, the symbols hard to make out.

The staff's symbols helped a song-stitcher remember her tales, as did tapping the staff on the ground. But Pippa hadn't heard *this* song-stitcher tapping.

Where had she come from?

"Hurt, child?" The woman extended her staff. "Here."

Pippa gripped it and rose to her feet, noticing one symbol in particular carved on the top. Three feathers, woven together.

"What does it mean?" asked Pippa.

"Ah," said the woman, eyebrows rising. "There are more stories coming soon for that one."

Pippa was puzzled. Weren't a song-stitcher's tales old ones, the stories of gods and goddesses? Unless this woman had seen something in the storm too. Had she seen Nikomedes?

The song-stitcher's dark eyes clouded over as she tapped her staff in time to her words. *"Aloft, wings beat and feathers fly. Hark the horses of the sky."*

So she *had* seen something! Or was she speaking in riddles, as song-stitchers tended to do?

"What tale is that from?" asked Pippa. "Tell me more."

"I wish, I wish. But that one is not a tale for telling— not yet. I can tell you another, a tale of great intrigue."

Although she was tempted, Pippa shook her head. "I must go back," said Pippa. Really, she'd already been gone too long. The mare and her colt didn't like storms, and she didn't want to leave them untended.

Not to mention, Alcaeus would be furious. Although he rarely whipped the horses, he did not shy from whipping her.

The song-stitcher's hand shot out and gripped Pippa's arm, her fingers curling around Pippa's wrist like snakes.

"No!" Her voice crackled. "There are so many tales I know. I know the truths of the gods. I've seen things no one should."

Pippa had heard of song-stitchers like this—those who had gone mad from their stories. Often they rocked alone in corners of the market, muttering and murmuring to no one. Some said that the gods had disgraced them, or that their stories were too accurate for the gods' liking, and so they had been punished.

The song-stitcher went on. "Share your food with me then? But you don't have any, do you? Only fate kept you alive, but for a purpose? We'll see . . ."

Pippa yanked her arm free and hurried away. It was simply madness and luck that this woman had landed on some truths. She glanced back. The song-stitcher was still tapping her cane. Poor woman. But Pippa would be in trouble herself if she didn't make it back before the groom discovered she was gone.

Already the clouds were gathered far off in the distance and the rain was nearly a memory.

The magic was over.

Two

When Pippa returned to the stables, Alcaeus was there, hunched yet imposing, in the mare's stall. "You old nag," the groom soothed. "Stop your fussing. It's just a storm."

The mare's colt, in the stall opposite, flicked his ears back. He, like his mother, was clearly agitated.

Pippa put a comforting hand on his neck. His ears relaxed; his tail swished. He had long lashes almost like a donkey and was one of her favorites. She stepped closer. Hay crunched under Pippa's feet, and the colt nickered. The groom turned and spied Pippa, his brow furrowing.

"There you are, useless girl! Where were you?"

"I saw . . . the storm . . . ," Pippa stammered.

"Yes, yes, the whole city saw," huffed the groom. His gaze drifted to her muddy legs and dripping tunic. "But what were you doing out in it?"

"I saw—" she started again.

He didn't let her finish. "You don't see, you do!" he barked, in a tone he never used with the horses. "And you aren't doing anything! The stalls aren't clean, nor the mare fed."

The groom paced, his fists clenching and unclenching over an invisible whip. "I should never have taken you on. A girl working with horses. Pah!"

"But . . . I saw a wing—in the storm. The wing of a horse."

His eyebrows furrowed again. "You think Zeus would grant *you* sight of his steed?"

"I-I-I" she stammered. "I didn't think . . ."

"Think! That's your problem. You think *too* much." His breath reeked of stale wine and sardines, and he stopped pacing and leaned toward her. "Always thinking. Trying to tell me which horse has a lame hoof. As if I hadn't spotted the stone. Of course I knew! My great-grandfather rode the gods' horses!"

The groom loved to boast of his family, but what was truth and what was wine speaking, Pippa never knew. She did know that she had done him a service earlier by letting him know of his mare's condition. If he had known about the stone in her hoof, then why hadn't he picked it out?

"You may have a way with horses, but as of tomorrow you no longer have a job here," he went on.

"Fine," the word burst from Pippa's mouth before she could stop it.

"Fine?" the groom spat. A fleck of sardine flew toward her. "I'm glad you think so, for now I want you out *immediately*. An empty stomach and no bed should teach you some manners. Believe me, you shall find no beds or stables around here, not after I tell my friends what I think of you."

"But . . ."

"Ha! Not so quick with your tongue now, are you?"

Pippa's heart clenched. She was good with horses; he had just said so himself. Surely he wouldn't lie to others—but . . . this was Alcaeus. Of *course* he would. She gulped. Losing her job was one thing, but not being able to work with horses . . .

"I see you don't have a response to *that*."

"I didn't mean . . . ," Pippa started.

"Well, stop standing there like a statue! I want you gone by the time I'm back from supper! Not that you have any belongings to collect, do you, foundling? Good riddance, though now I will have the bother of finding a replacement." He grunted and then left, muttering under his breath.

The mare nickered, and Pippa turned her attention to the horse. Although her head hung low as usual, the whites of her eyes were showing, and her ears pricked. The mare was used to the groom shouting at Pippa. It must have been the storm that spooked her. Pippa rubbed the mare's neck. "Hush, hush," she soothed.

She would not miss the groom's yelling. Or the stables themselves. Even her meager food; it wasn't like Alcaeus gave her much. But she'd miss the horses. She loved horses more than anything: their warm, moist breath; their thoughtful eyes; and the proud way they tossed their heads.

"Don't worry," Pippa murmured. "The storm is over now."

It was true—the night sky was clear and strewn with stars.

Chewing on a handful of horse grain—who knew

when she might eat next—she climbed, one last time, to the stables' roof. The tiles were slippery as eels, so she was careful but not afraid.

The roof was her favorite place. From there, she could see the whole city and the great temple, the Parthenon, in the distance. Sometimes, with the stars and moon so close and the horses below, she felt like a goddess up on Mount Olympus. Though a goddess wouldn't be forced to eat animal feed.

Pippa gazed at the sky. Of all the families of stars, Pegasus seemed to jump from the darkness, each star twinkling doubly as bright.

How many nights had she hoped to spot a winged horse among the twinkling stars? Today, had she really seen one? Already the storm seemed like ages ago.

Pippa took a deep breath. She shouldn't have wandered from the stables. But it was too late for regrets. Alcaeus's heart was shriveled like a fig without any of the sweetness. There was nothing she could do except go into Athens tomorrow and beg. It would be harder now that she was almost twelve; people wouldn't be as generous as when she was younger. And there were slave catchers too, always on the lookout for a foundling.

To comfort herself, Pippa reached for the coin tucked in her pocket. It was thin, thinner than most coins, and the symbol on it was almost worn away from rubbing. A winged horse. She liked to feel the shape beneath her fingers.

Once, a stable boy she'd worked with had told her the coin was an *obolos*, a special token used to pay the ferryman to carry you across the river Styx into the Underworld after you died. Perhaps it was. After all, her parents had left her by a well when she was a baby, with nothing more than this coin.

Lots of babies were abandoned—sometimes because a family was poor, sometimes because they already had too many girls. Whatever the reason, the baby was unwanted. She didn't know why her parents had left her. But if they had given her an obolos, they must have thought she would die.

Even though it hurt to imagine this, having the coin gave her strength. Because, despite everything, she had survived.

Though life had never been easy, there always seemed to be someone who took her in, sometimes for months, sometimes for just a few weeks. Her skill with horses had served her well. She'd always managed to find work—from mucking stables to helping a bridle maker. But if Alcaeus was true to his word, would she find another job with horses? Would she have to work in the mines . . . or clear rocks for ditches . . . or look after kennel dogs . . . ? A knot formed in her stomach.

Pippa gulped, and the gulp became a yawn. The night had a heaviness about it, like a woolen blanket. It was time to leave. Time to find a place to sleep—though where, she wasn't sure. She was about to climb down off the roof when she heard a voice below and stayed where she was.

"Tonight's the night," Alcaeus said. "The signs are all there. It's been near a hundred years. The storm was Nikomedes's farewell. Soon the gods and goddesses will descend and take their chosen children."

Children? Had Pippa heard him right?

"Humph," replied the groom's friend. "They'd be better off choosing those who know how to ride—like me."

"The best rider is someone light, someone small. A child. I've told you that, Gurgos. My great-grandfather rode when he was ten. Better he hadn't and I wouldn't be cursed as I am."

"You can't blame your luckless life on that."

"Can't I?" replied Alcaeus. "If he'd won, it would be a different matter, but he lost. . . . If only I'd had a chance. I would have won, I know it."

Gurgos grunted.

"It's time to sleep, for both of us," replied Alcaeus. "We'll see if I'm right, soon enough. The announcement will be . . ."

Alcaeus's voice went low, and Pippa leaned closer, until . . . her foot slipped out from under her. She skidded down the slippery tiles and off the side of the roof.

Thud! She landed in a heap on the wet muck below, barely avoiding the wooden bench on which the two grooms sat.

"You?" Alcaeus grimaced.

Beside him, his friend with a bushy beard frowned. "This is your charge? The foundling?"

"No longer a charge of mine," Alcaeus said, glaring at Pippa and grabbing her arm. "Didn't I tell you to leave?"

Pippa scrambled to her feet as Alcaeus dragged her across the courtyard.

"*Out!*" He shoved her toward the front gate. She stumbled but didn't fall again. She didn't look back, even though she could still hear the groom's voice:

"Serves me right for taking pity on her."

"You are too nice," came Gurgos's voice. "What do you think she heard?"

"What does it matter?" They laughed, and their voices faded as they headed back inside.

What did *I hear?* she wondered as she stumbled down the dark road. The song of the cicadas filled the air with a hum. What announcement?

This was one of the things she loved about horses. They didn't keep secrets. Not that it mattered, as the grooms had said. What mattered tonight was to find a place to sleep. With every step it felt like she was moving through honey. Had Morpheus, god of dreams, put a spell upon the night? It certainly felt so, for Pippa didn't make it far before exhaustion overcame her. She curled up by the side of the road, sheltered by a wild rosebush, too tired to care about its thorny branches. All that mattered was closing her eyes so she could forget the day ever happened and dream that everything could be different.

Three

A soft nose brushed her cheek, followed by a whispering whinny. She blinked. Was there a horse standing over her? Yes, with eyes black as the space between the stars but just as full of dreams. Then a face, this time a woman's, so kind and sweet she thought at first it might be her mother's. But it glimmered with a golden light. A goddess! The goddess leaned toward the horse and murmured, "If you wish, little one."

A sharp whistle, like a high-pitched whinny, split the air, and the dream disappeared. Pippa jerked upright.

But even though her eyes were open, she wasn't sure whether she was truly awake.

Instead of her usual bed of hay, she was lying on smooth painted tiles. The scent of laurel filled the air. Had she stumbled here last night? She'd been so tired—but she remembered curling up under some bushes in the mud. Not on tiles. Especially not ones so finely painted as these. Slowly she rubbed her eyes and gazed around.

She was lying in the middle of the most extraordinary, most enormous courtyard she'd ever seen. The early-morning sun shone above, and the walls of the courtyard shone back. They weren't made of sun-dried brick—but gold! A well gurgled beside a winding staircase, and the scent of laurel came from the enormous trees that grew in each corner—laurel trees, the trees of victory.

But, strangest of all, Pippa was surrounded by almost a dozen other children. They were all around her age but with oiled skin and brushed hair and dressed in clean tunics, ones specially for sleeping. Pippa had only one tunic. She was suddenly aware that it was crusted in mud from the day before. Mud had dried on her legs and feet as well, and it itched. She picked some stray hay from her tangled hair and watched it float down onto the tiled floor.

At her feet, she noticed a bundled-up red-and-blue *chiton* made of light linen, along with a matching belt. On top of the fancy tunic lay a brooch made of gold pounded as fine as a leaf in the shape of three intertwined feathers. She touched it cautiously, as though it might dissolve under her fingers.

Tweet! The sharp whistle sounded again, jerking her gaze upward. *"Get up!* Get dressed!" boomed a voice. "Get up!"

A huge man loomed over them, filling the doorway of the courtyard. He was triple the size of any man Pippa had ever seen. His face was lined with wrinkles, and he leaned on a cane. But his muscled shoulders and arms were those of a hero. The silver clasp on his red cape bore the same strange symbol—three intertwined feathers—as the brooch. Everyone stared at him in awe, as they scrambled to their feet.

"Who . . . who are you?" whispered a boy with long wavy hair.

"Are you a god?" demanded another, his nose as sharp and pointed as his voice.

The huge man threw back his head and laughed.

"Ha! A god! Now wouldn't that be fine? No, no god am I. I am Bellerophon."

"Bellerophon? The hero?" stammered a third boy, big as a boulder but nowhere near the size of the man.

"Hero?" replied Bellerophon, shaking his head. "Not I. Not now."

"But you tamed Pegasus! You tried to fly to Mount Olympus and you fell!" spoke a girl, the only one there other than Pippa. She was pretty, her hair piled on her head the way women wore it in Athens. "How are you here?"

"*Ha!*" His booming laughter rang out in the court-yard again. "Never mind me." He surveyed them. "*You* are still not dressed! Hurry up! I'll explain while we walk! No, don't take off your tunics. The mountain is cold today."

What mountain? Pippa's heart caught in her throat. But like the rest, she jumped to action, pulling the chi-ton over her head, clumsily fastening it with the brooch while whispers swirled around her.

"It can't be. . . ."

"It is!"

"But what is *she* doing here. . . ." The whisper, from the sharp-nosed boy, was directed at her.

He stared at Pippa. "Where are you from? Who is your family?"

"I . . . I'm a foundling," Pippa told him.

The boy sniffed. "You don't belong here. It must be a mistake."

The sharp whistle split the air for the third time, and Bellerophon swung open his arms, nearly knocking over two of the children. "QUIET!" he demanded. Then he pulled out a scroll and began consulting it, looking back and forth between the children and the words.

"Theodoros of Argos? Yes, you're here. . . ." The boy with wavy hair and watery eyes jerked his head up. "Sophia of Athens? Yes . . ." The girl near Pippa stiffened and nodded. "Khrys . . . Khrys . . . ?"

"Khrys of Argos," said the sharp-nosed boy. "My family has won *many* chariot races. Surely, you have heard—"

Bellerophon didn't pause. "Basileus of Thessaly . . ." Bellerophon glanced at the enormous boy, who shook his head. "No? Are you not he?" said Bellerophon. The boy reluctantly nodded. "Good," said Bellerophon. "And you're big too. You will need to be."

Basileus looked worried, but Bellerophon did not

elaborate. He just continued with his list, "Timon . . . of . . . hmmm . . . It doesn't say. I'll have to ask about that . . ." A slight, shadow of a child appeared beside Pippa, so suddenly she shivered.

The list went on . . . but her name wasn't called. Her brows knit together. Khrys smirked, whispering at her, "I *knew* you were a mistake."

"Hippolyta?" called Bellerophon. "Hippolyta!" he called again. He glanced around the courtyard. "Is there no Hippolyta here?"

Pippa jumped. Of course! It was her! No one ever called her by her full name.

"Even my dog knows his name," Khrys snickered, and a few others joined him.

Bellerophon didn't seem to notice. "Hippolyta, lover of horses. How appropriate," he said, his eyes twinkling as they met hers.

It *was* appropriate, especially since she did love horses, but how did Bellerophon know?

"An interesting choice," he went on, raising an eyebrow at her. "What a race this will be. Your goddess does love to stir up trouble."

Race? Goddess? thought Pippa. *What does he mean?* But her voice was stuck in her throat.

Not Sophia's. "So is it true, then?" she said, pointing at the brooch he was wearing. "Three feathers—I *thought* that was the symbol. The Winged Horse Race. *That* is why we're here."

"Yes, that *is* why you're here." Bellerophon moved aside to reveal the open courtyard door and a great expanse of green and rock and sky. "Welcome to Mount Olympus."

Four

Bellerophon did not wait to explain. He strode out the door, leaving everyone to rush after him in a swirl of gasps and cheers.

Mount Olympus? The Winged Horse Race? Everything was happening so fast. Was this all really . . . real? It *had* to be. The sharp nip of the wind on Pippa's cheeks, the sparkly brooch pinned to her chest, the giant hero striding in front of her, the other children scrambling to keep up. These were more real than the muck and the mad groom and everything down in Athens.

Meadows splashed in sun and dotted with wild-flowers rolled endlessly up the mountain. Below, Pippa could see rich green ravines and streams that snaked between forests. Her head was reeling with questions and excitement as she hurried after Bellerophon. She knew about the winged horses, of course—and Zeus's steed. But she had never heard of a race . . . except . . . The grooms! The old song-stitcher on the road yesterday! Is this what they had been whispering about?

"You have each been brought here by a god or goddess who chose you," said Bellerophon, his voice echoing across the rolling meadows, "for one of the most important of all the competitions on Mount Olympus, although it may be the least known. Which is exactly how I like it. The less mortals know of the horses on Mount Olympus, the better. It means less meddling. There's enough of *that* done by the gods and goddesses already." He continued, "Still, some of you have clearly heard of the race," he raised his eyebrows at Sophia and Khrys, "so let me set the facts straight. Legends have a tendency to twist things.

"The race takes place only once every hundred years. The winged horses live long lives, but even they need to eventually retire. The winner of the race becomes Zeus's next steed. Each god and goddess has a chance to compete, choosing a horse and a mortal to ride it—one of *you*."

Everyone around her stopped in excitement. Pippa's breath caught in her throat. So this *was* what the grooms and the song-stitcher had been talking about! This was how Zeus chose new steeds. In a race! With child riders! And *she* was one of them!

"And it's my task to train you," came Bellerophon's voice. It took Pippa a moment to realize Bellerophon had not stopped, and she and the others rushed to catch up.

"I am the groom of the winged horse stables. Although you will sleep and be served food at the residence, the stables will be your true home for the next four weeks," Bellerophon explained, marching ever upward. "That is where we're headed now."

"A month?" huffed Khrys. "No problem."

"Not nearly enough time, if you ask me. You will be lucky to mount today," replied Bellerophon. Even with his cane he moved quickly, and Pippa had to step twice for every one of his strides. "You might think you can ride a horse, but a *winged* horse is a different beast entirely. Just staying on until the finish line is a feat in itself, but the gods and goddesses want more than that. They have much invested in you. The race is very important to them."

He pointed his cane to a craggy tree. Or what Pippa *thought* was a tree. As they grew closer, she could see it was actually a statue shaped like a lightning bolt, as though it had struck there and stuck. The statue seemed to shimmer, as if it was carved from something other than stone. Words were engraved into it.

"*Nikepteros*," read Sophia, squinting up at it. "Victory in flight."

"Very good," said Bellerophon, stopping for moment. "This is the statue that marks the winners of all the races. But it is not the true prize. Not to the gods and goddesses. The true prize for them is that if their horse wins, they get to be Zeus for a day. Which is not always a good thing." Bellerophon grunted. "The year his horse won the race, Dionysus made wine tasting an Olympic sport, which, as you can imagine, led only to disaster. And there was that volcano created by Hephaestus . . ." His eyes narrowed and darkened. "And that's not even mentioning the side bets they make among themselves. Too many have been placed on this race already. . . ."

He stared right at Pippa, and she shifted, uncomfortable under his gaze.

"What about us? What is *our* prize?" demanded Perikles, another of the riders, sounding as haughty as Khrys.

"If you win, your horse will become Zeus's new steed, and you will join the demigods and -goddesses forever on Mount Olympus."

"I knew it!" Khrys proclaimed. He shot Perikles a grin.

Pippa's head spun. *That* would be her prize? Becoming a demigoddess?

Beside her Basileus whispered, "No, no, this can't be right." His face looked pale.

"Don't you want to be a god, Basileus?" teased Khrys.

Basileus didn't reply except to say, "I'm Bas."

Pippa wondered what Bas was really thinking, but before she could ask, Bellerophon strode forward again, past the statue. The slope was growing steeper as the great groom went on. "Of course, there have been winners who desire nothing more than to lounge in the gods' palace, but most have taken positions in the stables, caring for the horses and raising the foals.

You will meet two tonight at our feast," said Bellerophon.

"Tonight?" said Theodoros enthusiastically. "Will the gods be there?"

"Yes," said Bellerophon, though he did not seem too pleased about it.

"Who is my—" started Khrys.

"You will meet your gods and goddesses soon enough," Bellerophon cut him off. "But enough, for we have arrived."

At first, Pippa couldn't see any stables. All that was in front of them were cliffs.

Then, she gasped. The stables were the cliffs! They were carved right into the mountainside!

The stables were as magnificent as a temple, with a facade of columns as tall and thick as the trunks of olive trees. Wide steps led to a central archway. Although she could not see how far back the stables stretched, they were clearly enormous, two levels high. She had never heard of two-storied stables before—not to mention ones built into stone.

Looking closer she noticed the top floor seemed larger than the bottom one, with a row of windows separated from one another by columns. Or *were* they windows? They seemed too large. But what else could they be?

Sophia was eyeing the second level critically. "Those aren't windows, are they? They're the gates for the horses' stalls."

"Very good," said Bellerophon with a nod. "It is easier for the horses if their stalls are up high, so they can swoop out and fly back in. The gates must be left open if you are out on a training session, but closed at night, when the horses should be inside and sleeping."

Pippa took a few steps closer and peered up into the darkness of one of the stalls, trying to spy its inhabitant. Bellerophon caught her gaze. "None of the horses are in right now, they are out for their morning graze. They will be back soon. Come." He strode up the steps and through the stables' massive archway. The children followed.

The moment Pippa stepped inside the stables, she felt at home. Everything had been different and overwhelming so far, but this was familiar. The main room was filled with the sweet smell of hay and horses. Although she expected it to be dark, it wasn't. Not only did sunbeams stream through the archway, light poured in in dappled patterns from giant olive oil lamps hanging from the walls. In the center, water gurgled in a cistern. Troughs were carved into the stone floor around it. Stacks of hay and open barrels lined one wall. The barrels were overflowing with barley and beans for mash and rosy apples. Pippa was surprised to also see an assortment of nuts and seeds.

To Pippa's left was a doorway into the tack room. She peered in and saw a whole wall of golden bridles gleaming in the darkness. In the center was the shadowy shape of a chariot far, far larger than the ones pulled through the streets of Athens.

"Come," Bellerophon said, and led them farther inside. Behind the cistern, at the back of the room, Pippa could now make out stairs, half-hidden in shadow.

They must lead up to the stalls, she thought, trying to get a closer look. She jumped back in surprise when a figure stepped out of the shadows.

"So you are here at last," he said.

Although the man was as large as Bellerophon, he was much younger and more simply attired, with a short cloak carelessly draped over one shoulder, and he clutched a spear instead of a cane. He looked like he was glowing, and the scars crisscrossing his face gleamed as he grinned. It wasn't a warm grin like

Bellerophon's though. It seemed full of thorns.

Pippa noticed Bellerophon tense. "Although we are honored by your presence, Ares, you know you should not be here, not right now."

"Of course, of course," said Ares. "I just wanted to welcome the riders." Pippa saw his eyes flick from one child to another, before his gaze at last landed on her, taking in her tangled hair and muddy legs.

He chuckled, and his chuckle turned to a laugh. He was laughing at her, just like other children had. "Who chose you?" He laughed louder. "Let me guess, I bet it was *her*. Typical—following her heart instead of her head! What a costly mistake! Ha! I have nothing to worry about, then."

Having the other riders, like Khrys, say she was a mistake was one thing. Having a god say it made Pippa's stomach knot.

Bellerophon's face reddened too, but his voice was calm and controlled. "Here, all riders are the same. You know that, Ares. And now I insist," said Bellerophon, gesturing to the doorway with a tilt of his head. "The horses will be here shortly, and I must gather the bridles."

"Of course," said Ares. He nodded at Bas. "I shall

see *you* soon." Bas blushed, and Ares strolled away, still grinning.

When he was gone, everyone began to whisper excitedly.

"Did you see his scars?!"

"Of course he has scars. He's the god of war!"

"And he's coming back to see you!" said Theodoros, impressed, to Bas. "He's your god! He chose *you*!"

But Bas looked uncomfortable. Bellerophon too. The groom ran his hand through his hair. "Completely against protocol. I will have to speak to Zeus about this," he muttered. "Now where was I?"

"You were going to show us around," said Sophia.

"Ah, yes," said Bellerophon. "Of course. Feeding is your responsibility as well, so I will have to go over that. But I think, before there are further interruptions, you deserve to meet your horses."

Five

Bellerophon led the children back outside, and they lined up while he fetched the bridles. The sun shone brighter now. White clouds spread across the sky, wispy and long like horses' tails, but there was no trace of actual horses, winged or otherwise.

In the distance, Pippa spied three poles topped by glittering flags that were whipping in the wind. "I see you've spotted the flags," said Bellerophon, returning with his arms full. "They mark the training course."

He began handing out a golden bridle to each child, giving an especially large one to Bas. "Your horses already know who you are," he said. "They were there when you were chosen.

"All you must do," continued Bellerophon, "is slip the bridles onto them when they approach you." When he reached Pippa, he chuckled. "Good luck."

He whistled, a high birdlike call so loud that even the clouds seemed to shudder.

And they kept shuddering as the sound of beating wings—enormous wings—filled the air. A rush of wind blew across the pasture. Pippa held her breath . . . and looked up.

They were coming, silhouetted against the skyline. Closer, closer, until Pippa could see them properly. The horses!

Horses, winged horses, all different colors and sizes, swooped from the sky. Silver hooves, golden eyes, feathers that flashed and sparkled in the sunlight. They were like stars, if stars had wings.

All those nights on stable roofs, gazing at the sky, dreaming of winged horses, and now Pippa's wishes were galloping to greet her!

And then—all of a sudden, a monster of a horse plummeted from the sky. Its wings were bony and black, thrusting from its back like the gnarled branches of an oak tree. Its eyes were red, and as it flew, it tossed its mane and reared up, letting out a sound that was more like a roar than a whinny.

Was this her horse? It lunged and landed . . . in front of Bas. Pippa breathed a sigh of relief but felt sorry for the boy.

Bas turned to Bellerophon with panic in his eyes.

"Meet Kerauno, horse of Ares!" said Bellerophon.

"Horse? He's a monster." Pippa heard Sophia mutter what she herself was thinking.

Once Bas had gotten the bridle on Kerauno, after several failed attempts, the other horses began to land. As each touched down and folded up its wings, Bellerophon called out its name. A muscular stallion with sky-blue wings trotted over to Theodoros. "Hali! Horse of Poseidon," announced Bellerophon. Hali's mane and tail shimmered blue and green, just like the ocean.

The next was a slim black steed with wings the shade of a midnight sky. "Skotos, horse of Hades!" called out Bellerophon.

The horse swooped down and landed delicately next to the boy called Timon. They were a good match, thought Pippa, for Timon was slight, and Skotos seemed like he needed a small rider. Even though his coat shone and his eyes were bright, Pippa could see all the horse's ribs.

"I'm glad Hades is not my patron," muttered one of the children beside Pippa.

Pippa too was grateful that she wasn't the choice of Hades, god of death. But whose was she? And what was her horse like?

An older horse, the color of a great gray owl, flew toward Sophia. "Ajax, horse of Athena!" boomed Bellerophon.

"I am honored to ride for the goddess of wisdom," said Sophia.

Pippa could see an angry scar running down one of his flanks, and wondered why Athena would choose a horse that looked like he had been in battle. But when she saw how still and stately he stood beside Sophia, she knew he was clearly an experienced steed, with control many of the other horses lacked.

Khrys's golden steed, Khruse, for example, reared up as soon as he landed and blew dust into Khrys's eyes with a final flap of his mighty wings. The horse's feathers sparkled and shone, a perfect match for Apollo, the sun god.

But no horse landed in front of Pippa. She squinted

anxiously into the sky but saw nothing.

Bellerophon strode over to her. "Don't worry. I expected your steed might be late," he said. "He's always had his head in the clouds, that horse, from the time he was a foal. That's why his name is Zephyr, after the wind god. Zephyr loves to dally like the breezes. Still, despite his challenges, there is much to love about him. As Aphrodite well knows. Be patient. He will come."

Aphrodite! The goddess of love chose her?! She couldn't think on it for long, because Bellerophon whistled again.

Pippa squinted back up at the sky.

With her eyes fixed on the clouds, she heard the shout before she saw the danger.

"Watch out!" cried Bas.

Kerauno had escaped his grasp and was headed right for her. Pippa wanted to run, but she couldn't, frozen in fear, mesmerized by the horse's raging red eyes.

And then, from the side, came a blur of wings and hooves. A small horse darted in Kerauno's path.

A horse like a moonbeam.

Kerauno took to the air, leaping over the smaller horse at the last moment, before whinnying and crashing down like an avalanche a short distance away. Bas ran to get his horse under control, while the tiny horse landed in front of Pippa with a soft thump.

Zephyr was small and white, with floppy ears like a donkey's and black-tipped wings that rose above him like cresting waves. His eyes were like the tips of his wings, black as the night sky. His forelock curled up like a tiny horn. He looked strangely familiar. Where had she seen him before? *Of course.* He looked just like the horse in her dream.

"*That's* your horse?" Khrys snorted. Now that the danger was over, he had found his voice again. "That's not a horse. That's a mosquito."

The gangly boy named Perikles, Artemis's rider, giggled, and some others joined in too.

Bellerophon wasn't laughing, however. His arms were crossed. "And what do you think you are holding? Strings? Those are bridles, and they need to be put on your horses."

Khrys and Perikles quickly turned to their horses— and Pippa too.

"Don't listen to those boys," Pippa told Zephyr. She knew how it felt to be made fun of, but it didn't seem to bother the horse. He was eyeing her curiously.

Slowly, she reached out her hand and stroked his nose, his neck, and lightly touched his quivering wings, which were now folded on his back. The feathers were long and soft. Warm too. Under them, she could feel his flank rising and falling as he caught his breath.

"Good boy, good Zeph," she said. He snorted softly at the nickname, and Pippa smiled. He seemed to like her. Just as she thought this, though, he tossed his head and pulled away from her hand.

"Is something wrong?" she asked him.

Zeph replied with another snort and raised his wings slightly.

"Hush, hush," she soothed.

But Zeph tilted his head upward. Pippa followed his gaze to a bright blue butterfly that was flying up.

"Do you want to chase it?"

Zeph whinnied, and Pippa laughed. She looked around for Bellerophon, but the groom was busy helping Bas with Kerauno. Bellerophon had not forbidden riding . . .

So while the other children struggled to get the bridles on their steeds, Pippa dropped hers and grabbed a handful of Zeph's mane, boosting herself up onto his back. She settled herself into a comfortable position, with her legs tucked under his folded wings.

Without urging, Zeph began to trot. His trot turned into a canter. His wings spread open and started to beat. Pippa couldn't see, but she could feel his front hooves, then the back, lift from the ground. Her stomach lifted too.

They were flying!

The wind bit her cheeks, and she gripped Zeph's mane tighter and squeezed his sides with her knees. It was like a dream. But of course, this wasn't a dream. It was real, and she never wanted it to end.

The butterfly darted up into the clouds, disappearing into their whiteness, and Zeph darted after it. Pippa gripped his mane, wrapping her fingers around the coarse silver hair. The horse's wings flexed under her as they swooped, giving chase. Then the butterfly darted down again, and Zeph nose-dived.

"Whoa!" cried Pippa, her stomach feeling like it was a butterfly itself.

Zeph responded at once, steadying himself in the air so she could reposition herself.

"Thank you," she breathed. The butterfly was

gone now, but Zeph didn't seem to care. He whinnied happily, ready for their next adventure.

A sharp whistle sounded.

Pippa looked down to see Bellerophon, tiny now, beckoning them to return. He blew his whistle again. Pippa wasn't sure how to do this. She'd never had to land a horse before, but Zeph knew what the whistle meant. He whinnied, circled, and began to descend quickly. He might be small, but he was fast. Too fast!

Pippa wasn't ready and slipped up onto the base of his neck, losing her grip on his mane. For a moment, she was balanced there, between his wings, the ground rushing up at her. Her stomach dropped.

Frantically she reached and clutched a new handful of mane. Just in time, as Zeph suddenly leveled and landed with surprising grace. Pippa let out her breath.

Bellerophon was there to meet them. Pippa worried how mad he might be. But instead of a scowl, he wore a grin. He gave Zeph's neck a pat as Pippa slipped off.

"Now that was impressive," he said. "You have good form, but"—he looked over at the children who seemed ready to follow Pippa's lead—"there is to be no further riding until I have gone over proper techniques, such as landing." He gave Pippa a stern look and continued.

"And I must insist you all ride with a bridle. There are rules here, and they must be obeyed—for your own safety, as well as the horses'." He was grinning again, though, as he added, "If there is one thing Aphrodite is good at, it is matchmaking, and it seems she did right by you and Zephyr."

Pippa glowed and patted Zeph's neck too. She couldn't help agreeing and couldn't wait to thank the goddess.

Six

The rest of the day passed quickly in a whirlwind of wings and rules. At the end of the lessons, Pippa's stomach was growling like the lion-headed chimera. She couldn't wait for the feast to begin.

First, of course, they had to get suitably dressed. Back at the sleeping quarters, Bellerophon directed them upstairs to their rooms. When Pippa reached hers, with a rose carved over the entrance, she gasped. Surely this whole chamber wasn't just for her?

A gilt mirror hung from one wall, and against another was a wooden bed with feet carved in the shape of swans. Pillows, embroidered with doves, were piled high at its head, and laid out across the end were a chiton made of light linen with golden roses woven across it and a pair of golden sandals with wings on their heels. There were himations too—heavier woolen cloaks—hanging up on hooks on the wall. Beside the bed was a table with an oil lamp, a brush, and gold and ivory hairpins. In another corner, there was a bathtub shaped like a scallop shell. Someone had already filled it with steaming water.

Of all the finery, one thing in particular drew Pippa's gaze: a magnificent mosaic made from small flat stones covering the wall across from the bed. It depicted two winged horses, a dam and her foal, their noses touching in a kiss. Even though it was just an image, Pippa could feel the love between the two. A lump rose in her throat. She had never known that kind of love. . . .

She reached between the folds of her racing chiton for the coin hidden in her tunic and was relieved to feel it was still there.

Pippa did not know her family's name or anything about them, but for the first time she was close to some answers. She could ask Aphrodite. Since the goddess had chosen her, she must know about Pippa's past. Maybe her parents had owned horses. Maybe her father had taken part in the chariot races. . . . Maybe there was a good reason why they had abandoned her. . . .

But . . . maybe there wasn't.

Did she really want to know? She traced the wings on the coin and gazed back at the mosaic. The foal's wings were folded up on its back, but its dam's were spread wide, the wingtips kissing the ceiling. Tall as Zeph's.

"Lovely, isn't it?"

Pippa turned around to face a woman almost too beautiful to be real, who appeared like magic from the mist of the bath. Her hair was crowned with myrtle, and she wore a chiton dyed in lively patterns that seemed to dance around her.

"Aphrodite," gasped Pippa.

They weren't supposed to meet the goddesses and gods until the feast. But Ares had surprised them in the stables, after all, so who was to say Aphrodite might not put in an appearance too?

The woman turned to face Pippa and laughed, her voice like a chime. Black kohl lined her eyes and eyebrows, and her cheeks and lips were flushed. Gold hoops and mulberry clusters dangled from her earlobes. Around her waist was a tasseled belt that shimmered when she moved.

"Oh no. I am not Aphrodite," she said. "I am one of her attendants—Pandaisia, Grace of Banquets. Which is why I am here—to get you ready for tonight's festivities."

One of the Graces? If this was how the Graces looked, Pippa couldn't imagine Aphrodite's beauty.

"Come, into the bath," said Pandaisia, gently ushering her toward it.

Pippa had never been to the public baths, large pools where citizens washed and steamed—and even perfumed—themselves. She had only ever washed from a bucket of cold water. Now she understood why so many loved to go. As she stepped in, the basin's hot water felt wonderful—and made her forget her hunger.

Pandaisia gently scraped the grime from her back with a *strigil*, a curved piece of wood, which felt surprisingly nice. Pippa swirled the water with her fingers. It whirled in shapes of wings and manes.

All too soon, Pandaisia helped her out and into the fancy chiton. This time she did not wear her tunic underneath. The cloth of the chiton was much softer than the rough wool she was used to. The Grace fastened the three-feathered brooch at Pippa's right shoulder to keep the cloth in place, and tied the linen belt around her waist. Then she began to arrange Pippa's hair.

"What's Aphrodite like?" asked Pippa, at last finding the courage for questions.

Pandaisia laughed, this time a sound like a lyre being plucked. "Like is not love, but sometimes it is stronger. You must first like and then love."

"I'm asking about Aphrodite," said Pippa again. "I'm going to see her tonight."

"Tonight will come, but now is upon us. Here, the sandals." Pippa had never worn sandals, always going barefoot. They felt strange and stiff and pinched her feet as the Grace laced them up. "Now see yourself, child, and how beautiful you look."

Pandaisia gently spun Pippa to the mirror.

Pippa started. She hardly recognized herself, other than her face, burnt from years of working outside. Her hair, sun-tinged red, was piled on her head, her skin clean.

"Thank you," said Pippa, clasping Pandaisia's hands, then quickly pulling back, blushing.

The Grace smiled. "No need to be embarrassed. That is your true beauty. Your heart."

Pippa's questions about Aphrodite would have to wait until she saw the goddess for herself. Pandaisia might speak and move with elegance, but Pippa preferred straightforward answers. Still, it felt nice to be clean and wearing fine things. She felt brighter, taller. Pinching sandals were a small price to pay.

Outside the sleeping quarters, an enormous silver chariot awaited. Instead of wheels, two golden wings extended out from the sides, forming platforms so large they could easily carry all twelve riders.

The riders weren't the only ones in finery. Four winged horses stood at the ready, side by side, in two rows, as magnificent as the ones Pippa had met today, but regally adorned. Pearls were braided through their manes, and their tails were strung with golden threads. She thought of Zeph and how pearls would shine in his silver mane.

"I would have you ride up, except you are not ready," said Bellerophon. "It would only cause an embarrassment to us all. So meet my friends—grooms from the gods' palace, and winners of past races." He gestured to a boy on his left, who had a mane-like mop of hair. "This is Dion." Then he gestured to a taller boy, on his right. "And Archippos. They will take us up."

"Dion, the last race's winner," whispered Sophia. Sophia seemed to know everything. "He rode Niko-medes. And Archippos won the very first race."

"And now they drive the gods' chariots," said Khrys. "*I would be well suited to that task.*"

But they should be ancient, thought Pippa. *The last race was a hundred years ago . . . and the first . . .* But since the gods chose the age they wished to appear, the win-ners must too. Regardless of their age, they looked confident standing beside the great groom.

Everyone clambered into the chariot, onto the wings. Pippa climbed up too and awkwardly took her place between Bas, the broad-shouldered boy, who didn't even acknowledge her, and the slight boy, Timon, who nodded shyly.

Together, Dion and Archippos gave a shout and flicked the reins. The horses whinnied and their wings flexed, pearled manes flashing. Pippa thought of Zeph and felt a shiver of excitement course through her body, stronger than the rumble of hunger from her stomach.

The chariot jerked, and she felt herself almost lose

her footing. Bas reached out as if to help her, but he quickly pulled his hand away.

"Are you excited?" she asked. But he didn't answer, only looked away.

She turned to Timon. "What do you think the palace will be like?"

He didn't say a word either.

Pippa felt her cheeks go hot. So it wasn't just Khrys. Bellerophon had said that here they were all equal, but of course the other riders wouldn't treat her that way, no matter how she felt. It would take more than fine clothes and a glittering brooch to change her into anything but a foundling. . . .

The chariot lurched again, rising higher into the sky, and Pippa's excitement returned as they soared into the darkness, guided by the silver smile of the moon.

Everyone was quiet as they neared the top of the mountain and the silhouette of the palace came into view. There wasn't just one mountain peak; there were three. And as they drew closer, Pippa could see each one was decorated with a building—a spread of buildings, really, connected by archways and patios and turrets, glittering like clusters of constellations.

The wind bit at Pippa's cheeks, but her hands were clammy despite the cool night. First the extravagance of her room . . . and now . . . would she really step into the gods' palace? Feast with them?

Maybe not.

They landed on the platform at the bottom of the stairs outside one of the buildings. When they descended from the chariot, they were greeted with a rude surprise.

Although in the glow of lamplight Pippa could see the steps were made of gold and marble, they certainly weren't as polished or perfect as their distant shadows had led her to believe. Food was strewn everywhere: a pheasant bone, a half-eaten sardine, bits of figs and feta. Barley and honey cakes. Even a pot filled with beans. Not just food. There were goblets tossed aside and what looked like a smashed statue or vase.

Bellerophon seemed as confused as Pippa and the other riders. His brow was furrowed as he marched up the steps to the massive doors, which were carved in a frieze of the earth, the sea, and the sky.

He knocked with his cane, the sound reverberating into the night.

At first, no one came. But when he knocked again, the doors creaked open. Pippa tried to peer around him, to see who had opened the door, but she couldn't make the person out.

"I've brought the riders," said Bellerophon.

"It's not a good night," came a muffled voice.

"But it's the night of the welcoming feast! The gods and goddesses *know* this," huffed Bellerophon.

"Yes, indeed. But . . . Poseidon went into one of his rants, about how it should be a water race with the hippocampi instead. And Ares smashed Hera's . . . Well, you can imagine. I tried to stop them, but it was no use. You'd better come in. You can see for yourself."

Bellerophon grunted.

He turned to the riders and the two young grooms, staring openmouthed with the horses. "Wait here," he said. "I will be right back."

What is going on? Pippa wondered, as Theodoros asked the same thing out loud.

"A fight," replied Bas flatly. He slumped down heavily on a step.

"I doubt wise Athena had anything to do with *this*."

Sophia waved her hand at the litter all around them.

"Or Hera," echoed another.

"I'm hungry," said Khrys, almost in a whine. "We were supposed to have a feast!"

Pippa was hungry, too, but there was plenty to eat, far better than the scraps she was used to. She picked up a piece of bread from the ground.

"You can't eat that!" burst Khrys. His face twisted in repulsion.

"There's nothing wrong with . . . ," began Pippa, shame causing her cheeks to blush.

"*Disgusting*," spat Khrys.

"Disgusting," echoed Perikles, who was standing beside him.

"No wonder the gods won't let us in," continued Khrys, "with the likes of you among us. Foundlings have no place in the Winged Horse Race."

Before Pippa could reply, Sophia said, "She's a rider, same as you. And if she wins . . ."

"Wins? With that *pony?*" Khrys spat.

"Zeph has as much a chance as any horse," Pippa retorted, finding her voice. But the confidence she had felt earlier had disappeared.

"He's as scrawny and pathetic as you. Runts like

him don't belong in the race. And neither do *girls*."

Sophia replied, furious, "Calista. Elena. Damaris . . . Their names are carved in the statue too."

"Pure luck," said Khrys.

Sophia snorted. "I don't know why I bother to speak to you." She crossed her arms and turned away.

Khrys stared at Pippa. "Why are *you* still here?" He pushed her away, and Pippa stumbled, falling down several steps.

"Hey," called Dion. "Watch it!" He hurried up toward Pippa. "Are you okay?"

Pippa nodded. She didn't turn to look back at Khrys. She dared not. Her eyes felt damp.

"Good," said Dion, his face crinkled with true concern. "I saw the impressive show you put on today in the sky," he said. "Riding so soon, without any training. Well done."

A blush of pride replaced Pippa's blush of shame.

"If you're worried about the feast, don't be," he added. "There'll be food back at your quarters. Zeus won't want you to go hungry."

Dion smiled and gave her a wink.

There was magic in his eyes. Of course there was.

He was a winner—he got to stay with the winged horses, forever.

A door slammed and Bellerophon emerged, looking furious, and ordered everyone back on the chariot. The feast had been canceled.

Khrys grumbled and made a show of sitting as far away from Pippa as he could. Bas avoided her, too, but didn't say anything. Even Sophia, who had been nice, seemed distracted, disappointed perhaps.

But Pippa didn't care. She watched Dion and Archippos direct the horses back up into the air and down from the mountaintop. She didn't want to be with the gods anyway. Not really. She wanted to be with the horses.

She didn't mind if she was different. Dion thought she was talented, and that mattered more than what Khrys or any of the other children thought. Besides, the one thing she did share with them was the most important thing of all.

She wanted to win.

Seven

Late that night, Pippa lay in a bed far grander than any she'd ever slept in. But, as the Fates would have it, she couldn't sleep. The bed was too soft and the room too quiet. The mosaic across from her glittered, even in the dark. She was used to sleeping in stables with rough hay for her mattress, the snorting snores of horses, and the soft lullaby of their swishing tails.

I must sleep so I'll be ready to work extra hard in the morning, thought Pippa, rubbing her coin between her fingers, trying to quiet her mind.

But she was too excited—and worried. If she won,

she knew what would happen. But if she lost? She had overheard some of the children talking on the way back. Those who did not win returned home and were honored by their families for having ridden. But even if her parents were alive, they wouldn't know she had been chosen. She would return to nothing. Would anyone believe she'd been here at all?

She flipped the coin over and over, thinking of her parents. She had imagined every scenario. But even if they were too poor to feed her . . . how could they have abandoned their own child like that? Unless they had died. But who left her by the well, then? It was all a mystery. She rubbed the wings on the coin and gazed back up at the mosaic.

The tiles glittered so much it looked as if the wings were actually beating. Like Zeph's wings. Although she could not sense her parents—whether they were dead or alive—she could feel Zeph now, in her heart, waiting for it to be morning, waiting for *her*. . . .

Sleep came only when the sun began to soften the sky, and, all too soon, it was time to get up.

Breakfast took place in the courtyard, which had been transformed into a dining area. Wooden stools with feet carved in the shape of wings surrounded the space, and there were tables laden with food set in front of them. It was more food than Pippa had ever seen. Barley cakes, thick yogurt, spiced eggs, and all manner of fruits, fresh and dried, including pomegranates and soft figs. Although last night there had been a plate of food waiting for her back in her room as Dion had said, Pippa was ravenous now. Everyone was. She didn't pay attention to Khrys, or any of the other riders, as she piled her plate. She didn't care what he had to say about her eating habits.

After they were done, they bridled the horses at the stables, and Bellerophon led them beyond, toward the flags. Pippa had snuck a fig for Zeph but was now regretting it, as he kept stopping and nibbling her chiton trying to find it.

It wasn't long before they all came to a halt, and Pippa slipped Zeph the fig. They were still within sight of the stables, but in the middle of massive marshy meadows, standing by a tall pole with a sparkling golden flag at the top. The start of the training course. In the far distance, another two poles were stationed, each bearing flags that glimmered like stars.

"Circle all three flags," announced Bellerophon,

"and you've gone half the distance of the mountaintop, where the race will take place. You must not go up there, however, for the course is not marked yet. Nor may you fly below the mountain. Winged horses cannot exist in the mortal realm, not since my days on Pegasus long ago. Not since a rider tried to steal a winged horse from the stables."

"Steal a horse?" Khrys laughed. "What a fool!"

"Fool indeed," said Bellerophon stiffly. "And for it, he suffered. You must be careful not to anger the gods and goddesses. Another time, three children got lost in the fog during a race and weren't located until weeks later, down the mountainside, living in the trees with a group of dryads. Their patrons were so upset, they cursed them to roam the mountainside forever, neither dead nor alive. *Taraxippoi.* Not even the horses will go near them. . . ."

There was a long shivery silence. The whites of the horses' eyes gleamed. Zeph's nostrils flared. Pippa placed her warm palm on his neck. What rider would break the gods' rules?

"The gods and goddesses do not care what happens to you. Which horse wins is all that matters. You are expendable. If you trouble them or sabotage their chances, you'll most likely be sent home, shamed forever, or be made to pay with your life."

"Most likely?" asked Sophia. "Is it not certain?"

"Ha!" Bellerophon said, punctuating with a thump of his cane. "Nothing is certain here. Follow the rules and you shall have the best chance of avoiding wrath or whims."

"So this is the only place we can train?" Pippa asked, ignoring Zeph, who was back to nosing for more figs.

"It is the safest, due to the marshy ground. If you fall you shall not be injured—much. You may explore anywhere else. Just be cautious, do not get lost, and do not disturb the gods. Training used to take place farther up the mountain, over much more dangerous territory. This is safer, but still, you don't want to fall. And you should not, not as long as you heed my rules. No harming each others' steeds. No riding without a bridle. And," he added, looking sharply at Pippa, "no treats during my lessons."

Pippa blushed.

"Now, I'd like to watch you go once around this course," Bellerophon said. "This is *not* a race, mind. Merely practice. There is nothing to prove."

"Except who is best," Khrys murmured, too low

for Bellerophon to hear. Pippa saw Perikles—Artemis's rider—nudge Khrys in agreement. She rubbed Zeph's neck, knowing that she too had something to prove.

Once everyone had mounted, Bellerophon sounded his birdlike whistle for them to begin. With a magnificent whoosh, the horses raised their wings.

Pippa was surrounded by feathery walls, trembling and soft, delicate and powerful. Zeph did not take flight.

None of the horses did, except for Kerauno. He surged into the air, Bas clinging on desperately. Ajax, Sophia's steed, began to gallop toward the flag, refusing to flap his wings. Khrys's horse backed into Timon's horse, and it looked like the thin boy might fall. Timon steadied himself quickly though, and, with a flick of the reins, urged Skotos into the air. They catapulted up as though the horse was lifting papyrus, not a person. Khrys followed, Khruse's golden tail whipping out like a windswept flame. Soon the others were airborne too.

Pippa watched it all—because Zeph wouldn't budge.

His muzzle was lifted, his ears pricked, as though content to watch the other horses' antics.

"Come on," urged Pippa. "Come on." She pressed her legs into his sides, and at last he took her cue and began to trot . . . in a circle. "No," said Pippa. "Up, Zeph, like you did yesterday."

She steered him back on course with the reins and squeezed his sides again. This time, his trot turned into a canter, then a gallop; his wings beat, and his hooves raised off the ground. Finally, they were in the air.

Zeph swerved and tossed his head. He was clumsy and gallant all at once, and Pippa filled with pride. But she wanted to catch up with the others, and so she leaned forward, flattening her chest to his neck, feeling the heat of him, urging him on.

Kerauno was far ahead, zigzagging back and forth like a lightning bolt, allowing no one to pass him, though Khruse and Skotos were not far behind. Timon looked very calm, his body slightly raised above his horse's back, whereas Khrys was shouting at his steed and flapping his elbows.

As they passed the first flagpole, it took all of Pippa's effort to keep Zeph from flying up to nose the flag. "This way," she coaxed, directing him away with the reins. At last, after circling the first pole several times, they were on their way to the second.

Up ahead, Kerauno tore toward the pole. But he was much too close and—*whap!*—his wing struck it.

The monstrous horse spun to the left and collided with Skotos, knocking Timon sideways, out of view. Someone shouted. Pippa gasped. Had Timon fallen off?

She didn't get a chance to check. Loosened by the impact of Kerauno's wing, the flag caught a gust of wind, and, with a flash, spiraled up into the sky.

And Zeph—Zeph soared after it!

Up, up, up the flag went, glittering and sparkling in the sun. Pippa clung to Zeph; he was flying so fast. His mane streamed out behind him, and her hair did too.

Another burst of wind whisked the flag away and out of sight, and Zeph seemed to lose interest.

Below, the shouts continued. Had Timon been hurt? What was going on?

Pippa pulled at Zeph's reins, directing him back down to the training grounds. Soon she could make out Bellerophon and others surrounding Timon, who was lying on the ground.

They were the last to land. Pippa slipped off Zeph's back and hurried toward the crowd.

"You are lucky," Bellerophon was saying.

Standing on tiptoe, Pippa could see, over the others, Timon slowly rising to his feet. She felt a wave of relief and didn't even care when Khrys said to her mockingly, "Where's the impressive show now?"

"*Impressive?*" Bellerophon bellowed, turning from Timon to face Khrys. He waved his cane in fury. "IMPOSSIBLE! You *all* have a long way to go to be ready for the race! False starts! Hitting the pole! Leaving the course! And a *fall!* This is one of the worst practices I have ever witnessed." The groom tugged at his hair. "Go! Again! But this time, listen to me when I tell you it is *not* a race! You will race soon enough!"

The children climbed, chastised, back on their horses. Pippa rubbed Zeph's muzzle. His nostrils were flared, and his ears quivered. "It's okay," she comforted.

It wasn't his fault. The flag had distracted him. She had been distracted too. He just needed to learn to focus, and that was the point of training, wasn't it?

She looked over at Timon. He was standing beside his horse now, and although he seemed calm, he looked paler than ever. He *was* lucky. Would the next to fall be so fortunate? She gave Zeph's muzzle another rub.

No more treats, she decided. *At least, not during practice.*

Zeph snorted as though he could read her mind, and she added for his sake, in a whisper, "Not until we win."

Eight

Although Pippa was focused on training, Zeph, it seemed, had other plans. The more Pippa wanted him to practice, flying around the training course as fast as he could go, the less he obeyed. The flags were still an endless source of interest, especially the new silver one that had been put up to replace the flag that had blown away. Or Zeph would catch sight of a bird or butterfly, or a rabbit on the ground below, and suddenly change course.

Pippa and Zeph weren't the only ones with problems. Sophia's horse seemed inordinately slow and

stubborn, and Bas was still being bucked from Kerauno. Khrys's golden steed had taken a liking to flying
as close as he could to the sun, no matter what Khrys
seemed to do.

Every day the schedule was the same, problems
or not. After breakfast, Bellerophon taught the riders
a new skill, and then they practiced what they had
learned until lunchtime. In the afternoon, they trained
on the track, flying lap after lap after lap, until they
were racing the course in their dreams. By the time
they were finished grooming and feeding the horses, it
was time for a late supper and bed.

Bellerophon's morning lectures didn't seem to help
Pippa with Zeph, although she liked learning the best
way to hold her legs, so as not to get them in the way of
the wings, and how to keep the reins hugged close to
the horse's neck, so they didn't flap in the wind.

"Riding on a stormy day can be dangerous," cau-
tioned Bellerophon. "Since Zeus is the judge, he doesn't
participate in the race as a patron, nor does he place
any bets, so playing with the weather is his only way to
have fun. You must watch the skies closely."

Pippa did just that, trying to determine when there
were the least distractions. She tried training before the

lessons, only to find Eos on the horizon, pulling up the sun in her pink-gold chariot. Zeph wanted to fly after her, and Pippa couldn't blame him. She too was enraptured by the goddess of dawn's beauty. Pippa couldn't help but think again about Aphrodite, the goddess of beauty and love. She couldn't wait to meet her.

And, at last, the day arrived. "Come, hurry," Bellerophon declared, gathering the riders in the courtyard. Pippa noticed he looked harried.

"What about breakfast?" asked Theodoros.

Bellerophon groaned. "Breakfast?! I— Never mind. No breakfast today. We have to visit the gods. It's Visiting Day."

Ever since the failed feast, Bellerophon had said the gods and goddesses were planning a visit, but Pippa thought that meant the gods would be visiting them this time. "But . . . I'm not dressed to see the gods," stammered Pippa. "I'm dressed for riding."

"I haven't bathed in days," said another rider behind her.

"No time!" Bellerophon bellowed. "You have to ride. We're not going far."

"Not to the palace?" asked Sophia.

"Palace? Not this time. No, to the glade. Dionysus

helped me set it up. Not that I wanted him to . . ." He sighed. "Come, best we get there before they do. I've already brought your horses down."

And so they trooped out of the courtyard, into the misty morning.

"Do you think they will really come?" "What will they want us to do?" a few children whispered. Pippa found herself walking side by side with Bas. He was stiff and quiet, clearly as nervous as she was.

The horses stood at the ready. Zeph looked extra excited, struggling to keep still.

Pippa slipped onto his back. Bellerophon mounted a horse too. His own giant steed, with gray and white wings, that they had seen once or twice before. With a cry of "Follow me!" he led them up into the morning sky.

They soared away from the stables, and before long, Bellerophon directed them down to what looked like a temple. Except instead of pillars of stone, this temple was made from trees, each intertwining with another. And instead of leaves, these trees seemed to be growing feathers, silver and soft, long as the feathers of the winged horses. In the center of the temple a great spring bubbled up. "That spring was made by

Pegasus's hoof," explained Bellerophon.

Pippa stared at the spring below with awe. She knew Pegasus's hoof had power. Although her name, Hippolyta, meant lover of horses, she wasn't given the name because of that. She was named after the Hippocrene well, where the old song-stitcher had found her as a baby. *Hippos* meant horse, and the well, it was said, had burst into life long ago when Pegasus pawed the ground. She didn't know he had made other springs.

It seemed like a sign. She slipped her hand into her pocket and felt for her coin. She was ready to find answers about her parents—whatever those answers might be.

Bellerophon landed at the temple's entrance and dismounted, gesturing for them to do the same. Pippa and the others did so, and he said, "Let the horses graze. They will not stray far."

The spring and the temple were beautiful. Since the feather leaves didn't rustle in the wind, there was a quiet that was almost reverent. Even Zeph seemed to sense it and was calm beside Pippa. Not even his tail swished.

A crow broke the silence: "The riders are here!"

And with that, a flurry of gods and goddesses burst

forth—some swooping from the sky, others striding from between the trees, one even transforming *from* a tree. Each seemed more spectacular than the last. One wore a wreath woven of grains and a dress as golden as a wheat field. Surely this was Demeter, goddess of the harvest. Another had a scraggly beard tangled with bits of metal that glinted in the sun. Undoubtedly Hephaestus, god of blacksmiths. And it had to be Poseidon who jumped from the spring itself, splashing some of the other gods and goddesses and making them cry out in annoyance. Among these was Ares, in his silver helmet. He pointed his spear threateningly at Poseidon.

"Come! Come now!" bellowed Bellerophon. Pippa wasn't sure if he was shouting at the gods or at them. The commotion unsettled the waiting horses. Kerauno reared up with a whinny that turned to a roar.

"Whoa!" yelled Ares. He put down his spear and strode toward the massive horse. Gently but firmly, he gripped Kerauno's reins and coaxed the horse back down while everyone, including the other horses, watched in amazement.

"Oh ho! The mighty Ares without his spear," taunted Poseidon. "What shall we see next? Dionysus without his wine?"

Ares scooped his spear off the ground. There was a moment of tense silence, broken by a hearty chuckle. Dionysus raised his cup. "Never!"

Everyone began to laugh. Within moments, the riders had paired off with their gods and goddesses. Only Pippa hung back, between two trees, searching hopefully for Aphrodite. She knew Aphrodite was said to be one of the most beautiful of the goddesses, but all the goddesses were beautiful. How would she recognize her?

"This is for you," said a woman's voice, low yet sweet.

Aphrodite?

No. Pippa peeked around one of the trees and saw Sophia standing nervously beside a goddess with a long graceful neck and a high nose. Athena. Her chiton was short like the riders' and wrapped with belts that looked like serpents.

"Remember, Sophia, smart you may be, but I did not choose you for your wits alone," said the goddess.

Sophia frowned. "But . . . about Ajax . . ." She sounded perplexed.

"That's why I am giving you this," continued Athena. "Just like your horse, there is more than meets the eye."

She passed to Sophia a wooden box inlaid with precious stones, but her gaze met Pippa's. Pippa slipped behind the tree trunk, breathing heavily. She had not meant to be caught eavesdropping.

But it was hard not to. . . .

There was so much to see. Between an archway in the temple, she saw Khrys receiving a saddle woven of golden threads from Apollo, who looked remarkably young and rather aloof, like Khrys himself. She turned to see another goddess accompanied by a deer, pinning a long cloak on Perikles. Suddenly, the deer started and bounded away.

No wonder. Out of the forest emerged a fearsome sight: an enormous three-headed dog. He strode toward Timon and sat at the boy's feet. To Pippa's great surprise, Timon reached out and took a package from one of the dog's mouths. The dog gave an unearthly growl and disappeared back into the forest. Timon opened it, looking more ashen than ever, but he didn't share what what was in the package with the other riders.

Pippa had hoped that Hades would be there and she would be able to summon enough courage to ask him about her parents, if they were dead and now living in the Underworld. But she would have to ask her goddess instead. Still, neither Aphrodite nor any of her Graces—not even Pandaisia—arrived.

And they were not there when the Muses, nine nymphs, paraded out with platters of food, flatbreads and olive paste, crispy fish, spiced eggs, and soft figs. Music filled the air, played by Apollo on his lyre. While everyone enjoyed the food, Pippa stayed by two twisted trees that formed the back pillars of the temple. She wasn't hungry.

"Aphrodite will come," said Sophia encouragingly, walking up and handing her a honey cake.

"Has Athena gone?"

Sophia nodded. "Not all the gods and goddesses spend their time amusing themselves," she said, disdainfully gesturing to the others—such as Ares, one of his mighty hands on Bas's shoulder, the other brandishing a spear that he was showing off to Artemis. "Some have more important things to do. I am sure Aphrodite is busy too." Sophia sighed. As she headed away, she muttered to herself, "I was sure she would give me a scroll, something that would actually help me, but a box of medals . . ."

Pippa finished the cake and decided it was time to ask Bellerophon where her goddess might be.

Bellerophon, however, was in the middle of an argument.

"You know there are no tricks allowed in the races, Poseidon," he said. "That food for Theodoros's horse," he said, pointing to the seagrass Poseidon was holding, "looks altered. . . ."

Indeed, it was a strange shade of green, almost glowing.

"So what if it is?" Poseidon demanded. He shook his head, and water from his hair and beard fell over Pippa and the children like rain.

"It is not allowed," replied Bellerophon sternly.

"Allowed? Who are *you* to say what is allowed?" Poseidon's face turned blue. "What of Ares? Did you not see the spear he gave his rider?"

"Yes, but that has no magic in it. It is just a spear. Of course, the boy must not use it to—"

Poseidon interrupted with a roar. He flung the handful of seagrass at Bellerophon. It missed and spun toward Timon instead, but seemed to go right through him.

"Duck!" cried Bas.

Pippa didn't move quickly enough. *Splat!* The stringy, strangely colored seagrass hit her head, then dripped off, leaving her covered in slime.

Poseidon and Bellerophon just kept arguing. They didn't seem to notice Pippa. She felt a lump rise in her throat and hurried to the spring to wash herself. "I can't look like this for Aphrodite . . . if she comes," she said to her reflection.

"You don't have to worry. She's not coming," said Bas. He walked up beside her. His face was red, and he was awkwardly holding a spear. "Ares told me."

Pippa didn't reply.

"Did you hear me?" asked Bas.

"Yes!" said Pippa sharply, storming away. She'd heard. Aphrodite wasn't coming. Pippa wasn't surprised. She'd already waited so much of the day. She didn't want to stay there any longer.

Nor, it seemed, did Zeph. She found him nearby the temple, his attention fixed on a white bird, dancing just beyond the treetops. His wings were quivering.

"Okay, Zeph," she said. "Let's go."

Nine

Pippa slipped onto Zeph's back and let him follow
the bird. She felt the wind in her hair and smiled.
Zeph flew faster than ever. They swooped after the
bird, above a cluster of trees, and around a rocky outcropping. But when they reached the other side, the
bird had disappeared, and Pippa's frown returned.

What had she done? She and Zeph had just run off
from a meeting with the gods. Bellerophon would be
furious—and Aphrodite would regret choosing her
more than she probably already did. Unless . . .

We should go train, thought Pippa. That would show

the goddess how determined she was. And maybe if she was practicing, Bellerophon wouldn't care that she had left suddenly. But the beat of Zeph's wings seemed to sing to her: *Sunny day. Fly away. Sunny day. Fly away.*

The sky *was* bright, the nearest cloud far in the distance. Zeus had not played any tricks with the weather—at least not yet. There were no rules against flying around the mountain. And so Pippa let the reins slacken, just for a moment, and the sun crisp her cheeks. Zeph lazily flew along the path of a meandering stream. Pippa stroked Zeph's mane and lay her head on his neck, feeling his warmth and letting the wind whisper in her ears and then . . . something else whispered too. Music.

It was coming from downstream. The melody was faint but enchanting, full of bubbling joy. Who was making it? Zeph was clearly curious as well. He flew toward it, this time even faster than before. Pippa had to clutch his mane to keep from slipping off. *If only he would fly with this much purpose on the training course*, she thought.

The music wound along with the stream, growing louder and louder, leading them at last to a small pool. There, sitting on the pool's rocky edge, was a naiad, a water nymph. Pippa had never seen a naiad but had heard stories of their tricks. The nymph's hair, green as grass, was woven with reeds and fell all the way to her feet. Her skin had a greenish-blue tinge to it, not sickly but shimmering, and in her webbed hands she held a small flute, which she was playing. When she saw Pippa and Zeph, she startled and dropped it, and it fell with a splash into the water.

"Oh, I'm sorry," said Pippa. But it was too late. The nymph was gone, slipping into the water after her flute, disappearing as mysteriously as the bird. Zeph snorted, as though offended at the naiad's sudden departure, and Pippa laughed.

This was the world of the gods and goddesses—a world of surprises, where everything could change on a whim.

She hugged Zeph's neck tightly. It didn't matter that she hadn't gotten to ask Aphrodite about her parents. "You're my family now," she said, resting her chin on his bristly mane. "I want to stay with you on the mountain forever."

And the only way to do that was to win. She had to win. It was time to return to the training course.

With gentle encouragement, Zeph circled the

pond, then headed higher into the sky. It was then that Pippa realized the flags were nowhere in sight. Nothing familiar was. In fact, they were so far down the mountain, the meadows had turned to forest, clusters of bushes and small trees.

Oh no, thought Pippa. *I'm lost.*

Although she wasn't sure which way they had come, heading back up the mountain was a good start. She turned Zeph around and they continued flying. Still, there was no sign of the flags. Worse, the clouds had moved in and the wind had picked up. Now, of all times, Zeus had decided to play with the weather.

A hill rose up in the distance, like a coin half shrouded in mist. They certainly hadn't flown past these meadows before. Now she was sure they were lost. She peered down, hoping to catch sight of something she recognized.

All she could see were trees and grass and . . . a shadowy shape, flitting between two trees. Was it a dryad, a tree spirit? Pippa wasn't sure, but she was willing to speak to anyone who might help.

She coaxed Zeph down. Although at first he seemed hesitant, he eventually circled, then landed. Pippa slipped from his back and took a few steps away from him, toward the twisting trees. There was no sign of anyone anymore, dryad or otherwise.

"Hello?"

No one replied. Still, Pippa kept talking, in hopes it *was* a dryad, who'd hidden back in the bark of her tree.

"My name is Pippa. I'm . . . I'm lost," she added.

From behind her came an echo. "Lost . . . Are you lost . . . ?"

Pippa spun around. Three figures were approaching Zeph from the side. They were children, wearing knee-length tunics similar to hers. Were they riders too? She hadn't seen them before. They were all thin as wisps, with hair so fine it seemed to be made of spun mist.

Zeph's wings were raised and his body tense, as though he was ready to bolt into the air.

"Are you lost, winged one? Us too. Come, come to us," the children were saying as they came up beside him.

Zeph's ears pinned back, and he pawed the ground, clearly distressed.

"Get back," cried Pippa, rushing between the children and her horse. "He's not lost. He's with me."

The children's eyes widened at the sight of her, and

they gave a collective sigh, as though disappointed. "Are you a rider?" one of the children asked.

"Yes," said Pippa. "Are . . . are you?"

"We were," said the second.

"We are," said the last.

"Which is it?" said Pippa. It was hard to make out their features, as difficult as determining a raindrop's edge. She wondered if it was because of the fog that had suddenly swept into the clearing, or maybe it was something else.

"We were riders. Long ago. Before the race. . . ."

"We were cursed. . . ."

"We were lost. . . ."

"We are lost still. . . . Now, not even horses will come to us."

The taraxippoi! A shiver ran down Pippa's spine. Bellerophon had mentioned them. They were the children, neither alive nor dead, who had been punished for getting lost, like her. . . .

"Are you lost too?" one child said. "Are you joining us?"

"No!" exclaimed Pippa, stepping away. "I'm going back to the stables. I was just exploring."

"Do you know where the stables are? Take us,

please. . . ." The children grasped at her, their fingers damp as the mist.

"No, don't!" she cried, stumbling backward. She had to leave at once. But . . . where was Zeph?

He had disappeared!

Had he flown away? She glanced up. Clouds, dark as bruises, scarred the sky, but there were no horses. The children must have scared Zeph away. She should have been paying better attention. Pippa tried to whistle, but her throat was dry.

"You have no horse," chorused the children. "You are like us now. Come with us."

"*No!*" Pippa cried.

Her heart raced, and her feet too. The grass, wet with dew, licked at her legs. What had she done?

"Come with us!" the taraxippoi called.

"Leave me alone!" Pippa ran up the misty hill. Her knees were stiff from the day's riding, and she slipped.

One of the children was upon her. Her skin prickled as the child grabbed for her, this time at her tunic.

"Help!" she cried.

But there was no one to hear her. "Help!" she cried again.

And help came. Zeph! He landed beside her, still

clearly distressed. His wings trembling so much, some of his feathers drifted to the ground. The taraxippoi scrambled to touch them, even the one who had been grasping for Pippa.

"Winged one! Winged one, join us!" they cried. "We miss our horses. We miss our flying."

Zeph took a step back. Pippa jumped up and ran to him, leaping onto his back. "Go, go!" she said. He needed no encouragement.

He took off, the taraxippoi crying below them, Pippa's heart beating faster than Zeph's wings.

She didn't notice where he was going . . . until he landed.

Landed in a garden, beside a small red-and-white house.

Pippa glanced behind her. The taraxippoi were nowhere to be seen. She turned her attention back to Zeph. Her little horse was standing amid the bright vegetables, busy munching carrots. *Whose carrots?* she wondered. *Whose house could it be?*

The gods and goddesses lived with their attendants in the palace on the mountaintop. The nymphs and dryads lived in the streams and trees. The house was modest, even for a mortal, with whitewashed bricks and the vegetable garden in front. It didn't look like it belonged on great Mount Olympus at all. Had she strayed off the mountain? Fear nipped at her heart. But maybe the house belonged to one of the grooms, a past winner of a race?

Although she didn't want to get caught in another frightening situation, now, more than ever, she needed to find her way back to the stables. And the only way to do that was to get help.

She slipped off Zeph's back, let him nuzzle her for a moment, then led him to a gnarled olive tree in the garden and tied his reins to it. She checked again for the taraxippoi, but there was no sign of them.

"I'm just going to see if anyone is there," she told him. "Don't worry. I'll be right back." Zeph didn't seem too bothered, munching his last mouthful of vegetables.

The house really was very small, built in a horseshoe shape around a tiny courtyard. There was a cistern in the courtyard, but that was all, no sign of a person or otherwise.

Then she heard arguing coming from inside one of the rooms.

"Might!" snapped a woman's voice. "Might is

greater than love."

"Love!" insisted a second woman, her voice higher pitched than the first. "Love is greater than might."

"Not this again!" came a third voice, so raspy and low it could almost have been a man's. "And look what you've made me do this time! You distracted me, and I've spun the threads together. These poor lives will be a tangle." There was a heavy sigh. "Why can't you give up on that argument? It's best left to Aphrodite and Ares."

"But, sister, destiny depends on the outcomes of love or might, does it not? Just because *you* are the weaver, you do not care to trouble yourself with things that Atropos and I must think about every moment."

Pippa breathed in sharply. *Atropos?*

These were no mortals.

Nor were they gods or goddesses. These were the three beings who spun and measured and ended the lives of every mortal below the mountain. Atropos and her sisters, Lachesis and Clotho.

These were the Fates!

Ten

Pippa wasn't sure what to do. Should she go back to Zeph? She did not want to disturb them, but she did need directions. The Fates, she had been told, were as mighty as Zeus himself. They determined the outcome of every mortal's life.

She was still debating, when she heard a high-pitched voice from inside call, "Come in. Come in, my little knot. Don't linger. That's rude, you know, especially when we've been expecting you."

Pippa glanced around. She was the only one there.

"Yes, my sister means you. Oh, do come in!"

Uncertain, Pippa stepped inside.

The room, like the house, was small and simple. No mosaics or tapestries decorated the walls; no vases stood on elegant tables, nor were there fancy carved chests in corners lit by the dancing flames of lamps. Instead, the roof seemed open to the sky above, though it hadn't seemed that way from the outside. Was it really the sky? Pippa wasn't sure. In the center of the room stood a rough wooden table. On the table was a plate with a meager serving of fuzzy-looking bread and cheese, and a small ceramic amphora, likely filled with wine.

Two old women sat on stools at the table. One clutched a measuring stick, the other a pair of scissors. A third woman sat apart from the others, under the window, with a spindle in her hand and a loom beside her. Her fingers, though knobby, worked quickly, twisting and turning the spindle. But where was the thread? Pippa rubbed her eyes but still saw nothing.

"Ah! Come, take a seat," said the woman with the measuring stick, gesturing at a fourth empty stool. Her hair was silvery gray, and her face lined with wrinkles. She was draped in plain gray cloth.

"She doesn't want any of that food, Lachesis,"

snapped the Fate with the scissors. "Just look at it. Moldy again. What is the point of making food if we never eat it? What is the purpose of our garden if the things we grow aren't consumed?" She snipped at the air as she spoke, and Pippa didn't know if she was snipping threads or her words. If Lachesis was old, this Fate looked much older, so wizened even her hair was wrinkled. If the gods and goddesses, and even the demigods, could choose their ages, couldn't the Fates? Why would they choose to be ancient?

Lachesis looked at the bread as though seeing it for the first time. "We have food for guests, Atropos," she said, but didn't seem convinced of her own words.

"Our guests are never looking for food," sniffed Atropos. "They want advice and predictions." Atropos narrowed her eyes at Pippa and brandished her shears. "I hope that's not why you're here."

Pippa hadn't thought about it, but now suddenly she did. Did she and Zeph have a chance in the race?

"We won't tell you a word about the race," continued Atropos. "I know what you riders want. Not to mention those gods and goddesses." She clucked her tongue. "'Who will win the race?' they ask. 'Who will win? Who will win?' They should know by now that we can't tell such things."

"So much is undetermined, you see," came the deep, soft voice from the corner. "We only know so much." Pippa looked over at the spinner, who glanced up for a moment from her spindle and smiled. Her skin looked papery thin.

Atropos clucked her tongue again. "We know what we know, Clotho. And you'd think by now everyone would stop pestering us."

"Don't be bothered by her," said Lachesis to Pippa. "She is just grouchy because she prefers our rooms in the palace. But it is much more peaceful down here during the race. We really *can't* say anything about the outcome, you know."

"That's not why I'm here. I didn't know this was where you lived," Pippa replied. "I'm lost. That's all. My horse and I just want to go back to the stables."

"Ah, that Bellerophon forgets some of the simplest things. Didn't he give you a whistle? Some way to call for aid?"

Pippa shook her head.

"Hmm." Atropos tapped her shears on the wooden table.

"Oh, come," said Lachesis. "Surely we can give her

some help, a map, perhaps? Show a little love."

"Love!" scoffed Atropos.

"Do you really want another taraxippos troubling us? Disturbing our work?" Lachesis went on.

Atropos scoffed again. "I suppose a map is something we can share with her. Clotho!"

Clotho set down her spindle and nodded. She turned to the small loom beside her, her fingers twirling across the air between the wooden planks, like she was playing a lyre with no strings. Then she gestured to Atropos, who hobbled over and snipped the invisible threads. And when she had, a small weaving appeared. Atropos plucked it from the air before it fell, then hobbled back and handed it to Pippa.

Pippa gazed at it, dumbfounded. The tiny square of fabric was alive with detail, and movement too. The threads seemed to quiver. The map showed the stables and the training course, the sleeping quarters, and even the palace at the very top corner, as well as the hut where Pippa was now. "Oh, thank you!" she exclaimed. As she tucked the map into her chiton, her fingers grazed her coin. Surely, the Fates would know what happened to her parents—and that wasn't asking about the future, it was asking about the past. But before Pippa could say anything, Atropos waved her gnarled hand.

"Take it and be off. But mind you leave it behind when you return to the mortal realm."

"Atropos! Hush!" said Clotho, looking horrified.

But it was too late. The words hung ominously in the air. Pippa would be returning to Athens. She wouldn't win the race. She wouldn't get to stay with Zeph. Tears pricked at her eyes. The Fates might as well have snipped her thread right then and there.

"Now you've done it," said Lachesis, shaking her head. "And after that lecture on not saying anything about outcomes, too."

Atropos crossed her arms unapologetically. "Well, she can't very well take an item of ours down to the mortals, can she? Magic threads have no place there. I won't have any breaking of our rules."

"Breaking or *knotting*," replied Lachesis, eyeing Clotho.

Clotho smiled sheepishly.

"You *know* what I mean," said Atropos.

"My dear, please try to forget what you have heard," said Lachesis, turning to Pippa.

Her throat felt tight, but Pippa managed to say,

"Thank you again. I'll leave the map behind, I promise."

"Who knows if we are right in our predictions, anyway?" added Lachesis. "We are only three old ladies, after all. . . ."

"With lots of work to do," grumped Atropos. "And I've wasted most of the afternoon arguing."

Pippa nodded and headed to the doorway.

"That's not my fault, you know," said Lachesis. "You started it."

"Starting is not what is important; finishing is," grouched Atropos.

"No, it is the journey that is the most important," said Lachesis.

"Oh dear, here we go again." Clotho sighed. "Goodbye, child. And good luck."

"Ooh, and please take some of the carrots in the garden for your horse," called out Lachesis, as Pippa left.

Eleven

Pippa had never been the sort to cry, not even when a horse stepped on her foot. So when the rain began to fall during her ride back to the stables, she couldn't tell if it was raindrops or tears wetting her cheeks. Now she knew she wouldn't win. She would have to say goodbye to Zeph.

It wasn't fair. As long as Bas could hang on, he and Kerauno were practically guaranteed to finish first. But Pippa had so hoped that there was a chance. Now there was none.

When they reached the stables, they were both

drenched. Steam rose from Zeph's back. The other horses were all in their stalls, and the other riders were nowhere to be seen. Visiting Day was over. She should probably check in with Bellerophon and face her punishment, but she didn't want to.

Instead, she rubbed Zeph dry, then she sat in the hay in his stall and fed him the carrots she'd picked from the Fates' garden.

Bellerophon blew the whistle for supper, but Pippa didn't go. She wasn't hungry. When Zeph was done with his treat, he lay down beside her and nosed her inquisitively.

"I'm okay," said Pippa. "It's just that I don't want to leave you."

She stroked his mane and his feathers and slowly felt better at last. She fell asleep there, in Zeph's stall, with the map from the Fates tucked under her head like a pillow.

"There you are!" Bellerophon bellowed.

Pippa woke with a start. The great groom filled the stall doorway. His eyebrows scrunched together across his forehead like a dark trough.

Pippa scrambled to her feet, hay stuck to her sweaty

face. Zeph was already up. The sun streamed in, giving the little horse's coat and wings a golden sheen.

What time was it? Pippa's mind was foggy with dreams of stars and spindles, mist and maps. Maps! Below her feet was the map, peeking from the hay. Not dreams. She really *had* met the Fates. Her shoulders slumped, remembering what she'd learned.

"You certainly are here to stir up trouble—for me! You left during the visiting. You missed supper and breakfast—I was willing to overlook *all* that. But not morning training. There is a schedule we keep," Bellerophon barked.

Pippa didn't know what to say. What was the point to training now she knew it wouldn't make a difference?

As though the groom could read her mind, he said, "If you don't care to train, you have no place on the mountain. I will send you home at once."

"No!" The word burst from her mouth. Even if she was fated to lose, she didn't want to leave Zeph yet. "You . . . you said we could explore."

"But not miss meals or a whole morning!" Bellerophon pounded his cane on the floor. "Do you think you are better than my rules? Better than the other riders?"

"No! Not at all! I'm only . . . ," she trailed off.

"Only what?" A curious light came into Bellerophon's eyes. "My father might have been a king, but
I was an exile before I was a hero, and a hero before I
was a demigod. A little humility is appreciated by the
gods. But it was my pride and perseverance more than
my might that brought me here." He pounded his cane
again. The ground shook, and the hay shifted, revealing more of the map. Bellerophon noticed it. "Where
did you get that? From Aphrodite?"

"The Fates," Pippa said. The truth seemed best.

"The Fates?" Bellerophon exclaimed in surprise.
"Just what I need! *Them* meddling!"

"They told me . . . ," started Pippa.

"I don't want to hear it!" Bellerophon said sharply.
"And you should not listen either. The Fates speak in
riddles and have a way of getting into your head."

"But—"

"But nothing. Which is exactly what you should
think of your conversation with them. Did you know,
the Oracle said I would make nothing of my life; that
I would be a great disappointment to my family, to
myself. I could have listened to her. I didn't."

"But that's the Oracle, not the Fates."

"Pah! Close enough."

"So . . . you think I have a chance?" The words slipped out, though they were meant more for herself.

"Only if *you* think you do."

Her cheeks flushed with hope.

"And if you train."

The great groom scooped the map up with the end of his cane and flung it through the air toward Pippa. She awkwardly caught it.

"Perhaps the Fates gave you this map for a reason. On it, you will find a cliff shaped like a lightning bolt. It is the spot of the old training course. The old training course is more dangerous to fly, but it is truer to the actual course, which will be on the mountaintop."

"So I am not punished?" said Pippa slowly.

"Training there is punishment enough," Bellerophon replied. "And I *do* expect you to train."

The rain of the day before was long gone. The morning sky was bright, the color of honey, as they flew across the mountain. Pippa, however, sat tensely on Zeph's back, map in one hand and a fistful of reins in the other. At last, they reached the cliff shaped like a lightning bolt. Zeph landed at the edge, the sound of his hooves ringing out across the rocky gully below.

Pippa peered across the chasm.

A tattered flag waved on the cliff top opposite. To reach it, they would have to fly over rocks as piercing as the gaze of the Gorgon, the monster whose mere glance turned the living into stone. It certainly seemed like this might be where she collected her victims. Stones, sharp as knives, stretched as far as Pippa could see.

Zeph nickered. She gave his neck a pat, then slipped the map into her tunic so she could grip the reins with both hands.

"Are you ready?" she whispered. He flicked his ears. He seemed eager, even if she was less sure. *At least there aren't any other riders to distract us*, she reassured herself. And so, with a whistle, she pressed her legs into Zeph's sides.

Zeph jumped from the top of the cliff with a jolt.

Instantly, a rock sprang up in front of them. Zeph reared up, barely missing it. He pitched to the right. Pippa gripped the reins with all her might.

Where did that come from?

Before she could turn and see if the rock was still there, another seemed to appear out of nowhere, looming up and over them like a claw.

Just in time, Pippa directed Zeph down, though

one of his wingtips grazed the inside, loosening a bit of rubble.

Pippa watched as it tumbled down, down, down . . . She gasped.

There below, caught between two stones, was a bridle torn in two. It was blanched white from the sun, like a bone. And was that a real bone she saw too? There *were* riders here—the remains of them.

Distracted, she didn't see the next rock. Luckily, Zeph did, and he surged around it. But not before it scraped hard against her leg. Pippa cried out in pain. Warm blood trickled down her skin.

Pippa could barely breathe, could hardly see, as they whirled upward. She clutched at Zeph's reins and directed him higher still. Up, up, up, they flew, above the treacherous training grounds.

Only when they were far away did Pippa breathe again.

"Are you okay?" she asked.

Zeph's wingbeats, powerful and swift, seemed to answer yes.

But she wasn't. Not just because of her leg, which throbbed but would heal soon enough. But because of what she now knew.

She could never train on a course like that. The Fates were right. She really was going to lose.

Shaking, Pippa directed Zeph back to the stables.

That night at supper, the other riders looked at her questioningly. Especially at her leg, which she'd bandaged clumsily with her old tunic.

"Are you hurt?" whispered Sophia, concerned.

Pippa shook her head. "It was only a scrape."

Before Sophia could ask more, Perikles burst out, "So you're still here. I thought you'd been sent away."

"You gave up, as you should. Good riddance." Khrys laughed.

"No," replied Bas. "She's been punished. Didn't you hear Bellerophon say so?"

Khrys looked even more pleased. "Punished, hm?" He smirked.

"Which you will be too, if you don't stop prying," said Bellerophon, thumping past them to his own seat.

"Some hero." Khrys glowered. "He can't even walk without his cane."

Pippa had thought of the cane as an adornment rather than a necessity, but now that she really looked, she could see that Bellerophon's left foot was badly mangled.

She remembered what he had told her that morning, that pride and perseverance had brought him there. Had the injury happened when he fell off Pegasus? Had the Fates been against him too? She wasn't sure. But she did know one thing. Khrys was wrong. If Bellerophon had fallen and gotten up again, he was a true hero.

And she realized she knew another thing. She did not want to "give up, as she should," as Khrys said. She wanted to spend as long as she could with Zeph, and that meant she had to train, no matter how frightening the course was.

Pippa's stomach growled loudly. Suddenly she was starving. She piled her plate with food—soft flatbread and mashed beans and salty sardines—as high as Bellerophon's. And, just like Bellerophon, she ate it all.

With newfound determination, Pippa returned to the old course early the next morning.

She had a plan. No looking below. Instead, she focused on avoiding the jutting rocks. Although they weren't actually magic, they rose up in such strange formations that they tricked the eye, often appearing where they seemingly weren't before. It took all her effort and control to guide Zeph around them, sometimes even over them, as they sprang up in the sky like a surge of water.

Once, they didn't quite clear a rock, and Zeph's hoof hit the tip, causing a clang that rang out across the stony wasteland. He wasn't hurt, but it took a long time before Pippa had calmed down enough to try again. But she did try again. Round and round the course they flew, not touching down until Selene, the moon goddess, appeared, and it was time to head back.

Pippa was exhausted but proud. This time at supper, she held her head high and sat near quiet Timon and Sophia, who asked how her training was going but didn't pry.

No one else bothered her. Khrys and Perikles were too busy goading Bas, who was the one wearing a bandage on his leg this time. It seemed she wasn't the only one having trouble.

* * *

As the days passed, Pippa became a better and better rider, though there was no one but the birds and butterflies to notice her improvement. Although she knew it was a rule, she didn't always put a bridle on Zeph; she didn't need it. The leather of her sandals had grown soft now, but still, some days, she did not wear them, letting the winds tickle the bottoms of her feet as she flew.

The sky was her home now: blue ceilings, courtyards of cloud, and, if she was out late, stars so close and so numerous it was like they were woven tight as linen.

Sometimes Pippa looked for the Fates' house on the way back to the training ground, but the hut had disappeared from the map, as if they didn't want her to find them. It was probably for the best. She knew Bellerophon had told her not to listen to them, and she tried to put their prophecy out of her head. Instead, she remembered Lachesis's words: "It is the journey that is the most important." She wanted to enjoy her time with her little horse, for she loved him more than anything.

As Zeph skirted the stones with increasing ease, flying smartly and swiftly, a boldness billowed in Pippa. After a day of particularly fine riding, she'd watch their shadows, hers and Zeph's, race on the ground below, and imagine them winning.

"*Nikepteros*," she whispered. "Victory in flight."

Twelve

Pippa never encountered another rider on the mountain. Until one day, she decided to return to the stream where she had seen the nymph playing. Using the Fates' map, she reached the spot, only to find Theodoros there, kneeling on the bank, his horse in the water and surrounded by nymphs.

Upon seeing Zeph and Pippa, the nymphs dove underwater and Pippa could see ripples on the surface as they swam away.

Theodoros went red, tugging at his horse, Hali. Hali seemed to be chewing something and didn't budge. Theodoros gave Hali's reins another yank. "Come on," he barked. This was the first time Pippa had heard him raise his voice.

"I won't say anything if you don't," he said to her, finally drawing Hali out of the water and mounting his steed.

"But . . . ," said Pippa, confused. The others knew she was being punished and had to train on the mountain. *She* didn't have secrets. But clearly Theodoros did.

"I have to do this, okay? It's Poseidon's orders. Please don't say anything." He gave her a desperate look.

About what?

After he sped away, Pippa noticed strange green reeds floating in the water where Hali had been. They looked like the same kind Poseidon had thrown on her, food Bellerophon had forbidden. But when she went to take a closer look, they disappeared under the water. Should she tell Bellerophon? But she had no proof. And Theodoros had looked so afraid. She wished she could ask Aphrodite for advice. But still her goddess hadn't made an appearance.

If Bellerophon had told Aphrodite that Pippa had gotten into trouble and was now training elsewhere, it clearly hadn't bothered the goddess, at least not enough to come and seek her out.

Instead of worrying about Theodoros and Hali—or Aphrodite—she focused her attention on Zeph, spending more and more time with him.

She was spending all her nights in his stall. Her room in the sleeping quarters was beautiful, but uncomfortable—and lonely. She preferred the company of horses to a soft mattress. Used to years of sleeping curled on a hay bed, with the familiar snorts and swishes of the horses, Pippa slept much better in the stables.

Since Zeph's and Kerauno's stalls were side by side, Pippa saw Bas more than any of the others. Kerauno's stall was cavernous, double the size of Zeph's, because it needed to be, and Bas was often there late into the night cleaning it. Once or twice, he'd given Zeph a treat that Kerauno had refused. Not even sweets softened the monstrous horse, though Zeph certainly seemed grateful to Bas.

So when Pippa was woken one night by a cry of frustration, she thought it must be Bas. But it wasn't.

Pippa peeked out of Zeph's stall and discovered, to her surprise, that it was Sophia.

Sophia was standing in the doorway of Ajax's stall,

on the other side of Kerauno's, her hands clenched into fists, her body stiff as stone. But only for a moment, because the next instant, she slumped down to the hay-covered floor.

Zeph was still asleep, his folded wings rising and falling in a steady rhythm. Pippa tiptoed out of the stall and into the hallway, toward Sophia.

"Are you all right?" Pippa asked.

Sophia stood up, startled, brushing herself off. "Oh!" she said. "It's you. I didn't know anyone else was here." Her tone seemed disdainful, but then she said, "You're always here, aren't you? Khrys says you're sleeping with the horses now because you don't know how to use a bed. That boy has the arrogance of a god but the wits of a squid."

Pippa laughed, and Sophia seemed pleased at her reaction.

"He is exactly the kind of boy I've been warned about," Sophia went on. "Not that I completely blame him. When girls are only trained to stay in the house, and boys trained to believe that they are better than girls, it is no wonder. But look at us. The gods and goddesses know that we can fly and ride and do so much more!" She smiled at Pippa, and Pippa smiled back at the compliment.

"But I will have no chance of winning, not at this rate." Sophia sighed.

"What do you mean?"

Sophia gestured to Ajax, who was standing away from her, pressed against one wall.

"Ajax is sick, and I can't determine the cause."

"Sick?" Pippa stepped closer to get a better look, but the gray horse didn't seem to notice her. His eyes were dull and he looked gaunt.

"It does look like something is wrong with him," agreed Pippa. She realized she hadn't seen him grazing with the other horses at the end of the day.

"But what?" said Sophia. "I've checked his feet and hooves. There's no lameness. I've examined his wings, which seem strong and sure. He doesn't have colic or mange, for he is not sweating or itching. He has no fever, and he can stand and fly." Sophia sighed again. "I've done everything I can, yet he is not alert. He barely eats, barely flies. I'll never race at this rate!"

"May I look?" Pippa asked.

Sophia nodded. "Though I don't expect you to find anything."

Pippa entered the stall. Ajax's head hung low. She

crouched down beside him and carefully checked his teeth. They were worn flat, a sign he was very old. *Was he too old to be a racer?* she wondered. But when she stood and checked his wings, she thought again. They were strong, despite his age. Ajax shifted away from her touch, revealing the scar, wide and white, on his flank.

"I've checked that too, of course," said Sophia, leaning over Pippa's shoulder. "It's a wound from long ago and has healed perfectly. It should not be paining him."

"Was it from another race?" asked Pippa, as she stroked the horse's silvery mane.

"No," said Sophia. "This is his first. Athena told me Ajax was not always a winged horse. He was named after a Trojan warrior and was once a mighty battle horse in Sparta. That's where he received that scar. Athena heard of his bravery and prowess and rewarded him with wings. She was confident that he would fly as fast as he galloped, but he has yet to show any ability at all. When I tried to ask Athena what to do, she gave me this instead." Sophia pointed to a box in a corner of the stall. "Inside are his old war medallions. Useless. A scroll would have been much more help."

As Pippa listened, she stroked Ajax's bowed neck. She thought of the mare she had looked after back in Athens, who was afraid of storms and whose head hung similarly. She was a beautiful horse, fit to pull a chariot, but pulling a cart to market instead. Her bowed neck wasn't from an accident or hard work but from a broken spirit.

"Perhaps he is hurt inside," Pippa suggested.

"A stomach ailment would cause fever and sweating. I've checked that," replied Sophia.

"No, I mean . . . maybe he misses being a battle horse. You said he was great—brave and revered? Perhaps he feels like this is . . . less—"

Sophia cut her off. "Ridiculous! Here he has wings! Here he is on the mountain of the gods!"

"But it's not quite the same as being in a battle, is it?" said Pippa. She walked over and picked up the box and opened it. Inside were a gold laurel leaf and a silver medallion, like her coin but much bigger. "Maybe these aren't for you. Maybe they're for Ajax. To remind him of who he was. Of who he *is*."

Sophia scowled and took the box, snapping it shut. "I think it's time for you to go."

"It was just an idea," said Pippa quietly. She left the

stall, glancing back at Ajax, hoping that Sophia would find a way to help him.

Zeph was her concern, not Ajax. She didn't want to stir up trouble. After all, she had been warned.

Thirteen

As much as Pippa wanted to avoid the other riders—
and trouble—she couldn't.

It was a sunny afternoon, and Pippa and Zeph were
flying down the southern slopes of the mountain. They
were passing over a craggy cliff when, to Pippa's surprise, she noticed someone sitting on the rocks below.

The figure caught Zeph's attention as well, and
they flew down to investigate. As soon as they drew
closer, it was clear the figure was a boy. Bas!

What is he *doing here?* thought Pippa. *And where is
Kerauno?*

Although Pippa had promised herself not to get involved, she couldn't very well leave Bas there by himself. What if he was hurt? She directed Zeph to land, and they did so at the base of the cliff.

Pippa dismounted. "Are you all right?" she called, carefully picking her way between the rocks, leading Zeph toward him. "Where's Kerauno?"

Bas didn't answer.

"Bas?" Pippa said again, when she reached him. Zeph nudged his shoulder, and Bas stood up, turning to face them.

His cheeks were flushed, but he didn't look hurt. Except that his eyes were wide and filled with pain. "It's just my fate . . . ," he muttered.

"Are you looking for the Fates, too?" Pippa asked before she could help herself.

"The Fates? They live here? How do you know?"

"Oh, well . . . ," stammered Pippa, remembering that they had made her promise to keep their home a secret.

"It doesn't matter," said Bas. "I wasn't looking for them anyway."

"Of course, you don't need them to tell you . . ." She bit her lip begrudgingly. Everyone knew he was going to win. She continued, "What happened? Did you fall?"

Bas's flush deepened. He was clearly embarrassed.

"Anyone could fall off *that* horse." Pippa added, "You're lucky you weren't hurt. Where *is* Kerauno? Did he head back on his own?"

Bas's shoulders tensed. "Please, just go away," he said.

"I . . . ," started Pippa.

"You can't help me," he said.

"Walk to the stables then, I don't care," she snapped, her skin prickling with anger.

She saw Bas's shoulders tense again. "I will . . . ," he snapped back, then he sighed and his shoulders relaxed. "I just don't want to get you into trouble," he mumbled. Then with a grunt, he turned his back on her and headed down the mountain.

"That's the wrong way," said Pippa, but Bas kept walking. "Fine!" She turned to Zeph.

What had just happened? Her skin still prickled, but she was more puzzled than angry as she mounted Zeph and they flew off, leaving Bas behind them.

Once in the air, Pippa let go of the reins, counting on Zeph to take her somewhere that would distract her. She rested her head on his neck. When she looked down, to her surprise they were above some stables.

Instead of being carved into the cliffside, these stables were an enormous structure built of honey-colored stone, with a red-tiled roof and wide steps that led to a doorway. There was only one story, separated into columns with gates. Stalls. But why were the stalls so low?

Soon Pippa understood why. As they flew over the pasture beside the stables, she saw three tiny winged horses, foals. They were half the size of Zeph, with wobbly legs and even wobblier-looking wings. They couldn't fly to a second-story stall. In fact, could they fly at all?

Although their wings were outstretched, they were struggling to stand. One was, like Zeph, white with black-tipped feathers, and two were the opposite, black with feathers the color of apple blossoms.

Beside them stood a boy with a flop of mane-like hair that Pippa recognized at once. It was Dion, the previous winner of the Winged Horse Race. He was encouraging the one that looked like an even tinier Zeph. "You can do it! Come on, Aurae!"

The foal Aurae beat her wings furiously. Her hooves lifted.

"That's it! Flap, Aurae!"

Zeph whinnied his own encouragement, and they landed in the pasture.

Aurae turned her head in their direction and, distracted, tumbled to the ground. Dion hurried to help her, but she stood up by herself, giving a snort that sounded like a whistle.

"There, there, it's okay. Next time," comforted the boy, then turned to look at Pippa and Zeph.

"So we have company." He winked at Zeph. "Aurae is as easily distracted as you, Zeph," he said. "That's why I named her after one of the breezes as well."

"Did *you* name Zeph?" asked Pippa. "Did you train him?"

Dion shook his head. "No, I have been busy looking after Nikomedes. But now that he is near retirement and will soon join Pegasus in the sky as another constellation, I have moved from the palace and begun to work here. You will see Nikomedes's retirement ceremony at the end of the races, when the new winner is crowned. It is a dazzling sight—and a delicious feast."

"Oh," said Pippa, hardly able to imagine it. The race was only two weeks away, but time was passing so quickly. Would the gods and goddesses fight during that important ceremony? Surely not.

Dion gestured to the tiny horses, more legs and wings than body. "Some grooms like to push the foals into flight, but I prefer they take their time, learn their own way. Usually they are ready within a year. They are born much stronger than regular foals. Zeph, however, took a while to learn to fly, from what I hear. He liked exploring the ground too, as well as the air. . . ."

Pippa nodded and patted Zeph on his flank, imagining him as young as Aurae.

"These are the foals' stables, not the racing stables," a voice snapped. It was Archippos, the other champion. He stood tall and stern, his arms crossed.

"Dion, you know better than to invite a rider here. We aren't supposed to converse with them."

"I didn't invite her," Dion said. "She came on her own. And I wasn't helping her cheat, if that's what you think. Besides, you know that everyone—"

Archippos didn't let him finish. "That doesn't matter." He turned to Pippa. "As for you—you might have talent, but without training, that won't go far."

"I'm sorry," said Pippa, taking a step backward. "I'll go. I can find my way back. Zeph, come."

But Zeph was no longer beside her. He was trotting

next to little Aurae, who, a moment later, began to beat her wings furiously, and, one hoof after another, lifted from the earth. Aurae was flying! Zeph skimmed the ground next to her.

"Huzzah!" cried Dion and Archippos, clapping each other on the back, and Pippa too.

"Huzzah!" Pippa cried, filled with joy. Zeph circled around the pasture with Aurae, and then they came flying back, landing in front of Pippa.

The little foal lifted her nose up for Pippa to stroke. It was so soft, like touching clouds. And for a moment, Pippa's heart lifted up, too.

But the moment was broken by a voice, loud as the crack of a whip. "What's *she* doing here?"

Fourteen

Pippa and the two grooms turned to face none other than Ares, who had appeared behind them. He frowned, and the scars crisscrossing his face pursed. In his hand, he held a long knife with a leaf-shaped blade.

"This is no place for riders," the god yelled. "Archippos! Dion! You are sharing your secrets! I shall have none of it!" He pointed his knife at them, and Pippa noticed it was covered in silvery blood. Her skin prickled, and she took a step back.

"She came here of her own accord," said Archippos, apparently unafraid of Ares. "We've told her nothing."

"Wait until I tell Zeus of this!" Ares stormed on.

Pippa could see that, like her, Dion was trembling. But Archippos stood firm. "Tell him what? About your monster, Kerauno?"

Ares eyes flashed. He slowly lowered the knife but still spat, "Better he be monster than butterfly." He gestured to Zeph. "*That* runt should have been killed at birth."

"No!" Pippa burst. "You can't kill the horses."

"Of course we can." Ares laughed. "And we do. What do you think I just came back from doing?" He wiped the blade clean on his cloak. "It should be Hades's task, but he is surprisingly squeamish."

Pippa's eyes went wide. "You-you . . . you didn't." What started as a cry came out in a stammer.

"Horses are killed in the mortal realm when they are badly injured," Dion said slowly. "It is no different here. An injured wing, a broken leg . . . It would be crueler to let them suffer. The winged horses are not immortal, after all."

Archippos muttered under his breath, "If the gods took more care with them . . ."

"Took care?" Ares said. "The horses should be strong enough for their duties. Not like that runt. He's useless. Too small to lift a chariot into the air. Not fast or focused enough for one of Artemis's deer hunts. As for battle? He would chase a spear into his own heart. Do you truly think that horse could carry Zeus's thunderbolts? He'd have been killed if Aphrodite hadn't chosen him, fool that she is. The only place he's going to after the races is the Graveyard of Wings. I will make sure of it."

Pippa pressed herself against Zeph, to stop her body from trembling. Of course, in Athens, horses were killed, by quickly slitting their throats with a knife, if there was no other way. She'd witnessed it once, the killing of a horse that had severe colic, and it was a terrible thing. She hadn't known, never dreamed such a thing happened to the horses here.

Ares smirked. "I've scared you. Good. Better you know. Not that you can do anything about it. The race will be won by me."

"You never know what the race will bring," chided Archippos.

"I do know. Just as I know this girl should not be here, at these stables. You're lucky I have changed my mind. I won't tell Zeus about this after all."

Whether from fear or anger, Pippa wasn't sure, but

the retort left her lips before she could stop it. "You won't win. Not unless your rider learns to stay on his horse."

Ares's eyes narrowed. "What do you mean. . . ."

But Pippa didn't stay to answer. She hoisted herself onto Zeph's back. He was agitated enough himself, and the moment she was up, he was too, his hooves lifting from the ground, leaving the god, the grooms, and little Aurae far below.

The last rays of sunlight were flickering across the meadows when Pippa returned to the pasture with Zeph, still shaken from her encounter with Ares. The other horses were already grazing for supper. She was surprised to see Ajax with them, his head held high, his tail like the plume of a helmet.

Kerauno was there too. For once, Pippa was glad to see the monstrous beast. He had returned safely. Bas wasn't there though, or at least she couldn't see him. Khrys was easy to spot. He was standing on the back of Khruse, balancing, showing off to Perikles.

"I wouldn't ride in the air like this, but my great-grandfather could," he said. "He was a rider in the Winged Horse Race himself."

"Really?" said Perikles. "Did he win?"

"He would have, except that he had a horse like *hers.*" Khrys pointed to Zeph and laughed. Pippa could hear. She'd had enough of his bullying and was about to say so when a voice came from behind. "Ignore him."

She turned to see who had spoken: Sophia. More trouble.

But it was just the opposite. "I want to thank you," said Sophia. "You were right. I attached Ajax's medallion to one side of his bridle, and the laurel leaf to the other. This afternoon he flew better than ever. He's eating better too." Sophia paused, then added, "I suppose not everything can be answered by scrolls."

Pippa was speechless. After a moment, she managed a nod. "Horses *are* very prideful, almost as much as people."

"But not as much as boys," said Sophia, rolling her eyes at Khrys, who was still balancing on Khruse's back.

"I think you might be right," said Pippa. She thought of Bas.

"I know boys well. I should, I was raised like one." Sophia took a deep breath. "I don't have a mother either. She died when I was very young. My father raised me like a son. I had a tutor, and riding lessons, and we even ate together. If I win," she added, "I shall be a scholar and study under Athena herself."

"You won't stay with Ajax?" asked Pippa.

Sophia laughed and shook her head. "But I suppose you would stay with Zeph?"

"Of course," said Pippa. It was important, now more than ever, with Ares's threat looming.

Sophia invited Pippa to sit with her at dinner. Pippa was grateful to have Sophia's company. It kept the terrible thoughts out of her head. Especially because Sophia seemed to like to talk even more than read, and she knew so many amazing stories about the winged horses. They stayed longer at supper than usual, until even Bellerophon had retired for the night. It was very late when they parted, and Pippa headed back across the meadows to the stables.

The whispers came from the dark, near the lightning-shaped statue, which was now illuminated by the stars and looked like it was glowing with a light of its own.

"This is where my name belongs, and you shall ensure its place there."

Although the voice was more sinister than usual,

it was still recognizable: Ares. Beside him, Pippa could just make out Bas, his broad shoulders hunched over. She couldn't return to the stables without them seeing her, and so she crouched behind a bush, hoping they would soon leave.

But they lingered, and Ares went on. "Now tell me, how could you have fallen off? You are the most respected young rider in Thessaly and the mightiest too, or so your father boasted. He must be a liar, only good at bragging and braying. Braying, yes! That is what he deserves to be—a donkey!"

"Oh no! Please," cried Bas. "He isn't a liar. He's proud of me—my sisters, too—that's all."

"Then explain to me again how you fell. You slipped off *where*? And how did Kerauno end up back in his stall?"

"I . . . I didn't fall."

"Ha! It seems *you* are the liar. What in Zeus's name were you doing on the southern slopes of the mountain?"

There was a long silence. Pippa held her breath, as curious as Ares.

But Bas said nothing.

"You cannot be telling me that you wish to leave,"

hissed Ares, and Pippa could imagine his scarred face, spit flying from his lips.

"I . . ."

"When you win, you will be a demigod! There is no higher honor for a mortal. You can still visit your family, if you really insist."

"But not live with them . . . Not grow up with them . . . They will all eventually die—but I would live forever," said Baz. Pippa could hear the desperation in his voice.

"*Exactly*, who doesn't want to live forever?!" cried Ares.

There was a long silence. Did Pippa want to live forever? *With the horses, with Zeph, yes*, she thought.

Ares went on. "You are only a farm boy, and I have brought you here, given you every chance to win. Do you know how much it cost me to secure Kerauno as your horse? No horse, or rider, compares to you. None. I have a bet on this race. Might or love. I will not lose. I will not have Aphrodite bragging for the next hundred years that *love* was the winner. . . ."

"But—"

"But nothing. If you dare try something like that again, I *will* turn your father into a donkey, and your mother and sisters as well."

There was a great crack, like the sound of stone on stone, and then . . . silence. Was the god gone? He must be, for all Pippa could hear now was Bas, sniffling.

No wonder he'd been mad at her when she tried to rescue him. He didn't want rescuing. He wanted to leave. He was homesick. How could he want to leave the horses? The mountain? But perhaps if Kerauno was her steed, she would like it less here, too. And if she had a family of her own . . .

I'll tiptoe away, she thought. *I'll leave him be.* But she had taken only a few steps when the ground crunched under her sandals.

"Who's there?" asked Bas sharply.

Pippa held her breath, hoping he would leave.

But he didn't.

"Who's there?" he called insistently. He sounded almost frightened.

Pippa slowly stepped into the moonlight.

Bas was sitting on a rock below the great statue, but he stood up. His eyes and cheeks were puffy and wet with tears.

"I was just . . . ," stammered Pippa.

"So you heard," said Bas simply.

"I . . ." Pippa struggled with what to say.

"Think what you wish. My father isn't a braggart. He is the smartest, kindest person I know. And so are my mother and my sisters. I miss them, yes. I don't want to win. I want to go home."

"Oh," said Pippa softly.

"That's why I didn't want your help on the mountain. I was trying to run away. I miss Thessaly. I miss my horses, my sisters, my mother's *tagenias*, with honey and cheese." He rubbed his nose. "You must think I am a fool, too, now."

"No, I . . ." What *did* she think of Bas? "I only wish I had a family to miss, like you," she said.

It must have been the right thing to say because Bas looked up at her . . . and smiled.

Fifteen

The day of the race was fast approaching, and still there was no sign of Aphrodite, though the other gods and goddesses visited the stables more and more, their voices loud with boasts and bets.

Pippa had so many questions for the goddess, especially now that she knew about the wager between her and Ares. No wonder Ares hated Pippa, and Zeph, so much. They threatened his chance to win. Why had Aphrodite made such a bet? So far, it had only caused Pippa trouble.

When Pippa asked Bellerophon about Aphrodite's

absence, the groom replied, "Be grateful. These gods and goddesses are giving me a headache."

But Pippa wasn't grateful.

"Perhaps Aphrodite is staying away *because* of the bet," suggested Bas one night at supper. "Maybe she doesn't want to argue with Ares."

Bas was sitting with Pippa and Sophia now, though Sophia was slightly wary of the boy. But it was hard not to feel sorry for him, knowing how much he missed his family, although with Ares's threat looming over him, running away was no longer an option.

"What bet?" asked Sophia.

"Aphrodite claims love shall win the race, whereas Ares bet on might," explained Bas, stuffing a barley cake into his mouth.

Pippa contemplated an olive. "Might makes sense. I mean you are strong, and so is Kerauno, but love . . . ?"

"No one cares for their horse more than you," Sophia replied.

"That doesn't have anything to do with winning though," said Pippa. "Besides . . ." But she stopped there. Pippa had yet to tell them of the Fates' prophecy. Or the map. She wasn't sure why, except that she was still learning what to say and not say to friends, and also, maybe saying it aloud would make it certain, maybe Sophia would insist the Fates were always right. Pippa preferred to believe Bellerophon, preferred to hope that there was still a chance. She *had* to hope. It was up to her to keep Zeph safe—something she was reminded of every night, when Ares's knife, with the silvery blood on it, cut into her dreams.

It was for Zeph, not herself, that Pippa finally decided to risk searching for the gods' palace, despite Bellerophon's warning that doing so could result in being disqualified or worse. There were only two days left until the race, and the final day would be spent on preparations. This was her last chance to have her questions answered. Why had Aphrodite chosen her? How did Aphrodite expect love to win the race? Could she help Zeph? And what about her parents?

Unfortunately, Pippa didn't get far.

She and Zeph had only just flown out of the stables when a giant black wing swept over them. Pippa ducked. "Watch out!" she cried.

"Sorry!" shouted Bas.

He yanked Kerauno's reins, trying to steer the horse away but without success. The monstrous horse was heading straight for Zeph!

Pippa had no choice but to land. Once she and Zeph were safely down, Bas landed too. He secured Kerauno's reins to a tree and stepped back, shaking his head. "I don't know what's wrong. He keeps flying to the left. He never used to have this problem."

The beast looked even more agitated than usual. Flecks flew from his nostrils, and his ears were pressed back.

Something *was* wrong.

"Here, hold these," said Pippa, handing Zeph's reins to Bas. "I'm going to take a look."

"No—" started Bas. "It's too . . ."

But Pippa stepped forward anyway, into the shadow cast by the huge horse. His eyes glowed red like coals but didn't give off any warmth. His gaze was hard and cold.

She reached up to check his teeth—which were sharp and pointed, not like a horse's at all—but he snapped at her. When she felt his legs, he kicked out. As she touched his wings, he opened them forcefully. She ducked just in time.

"Are you okay?" asked Bas.

"Yes," she replied. Kerauno's wings spread above

her like the limbs of a tree. "I think I see something."

There was a gap in the feathers on Kerauno's left wingtip, like a missing tooth.

Carefully, Pippa crept toward the wingtip, concerned the horse might close his wings on her at any moment.

The gap was not because any flight feathers were missing. The feathers were there but stuck together. They were pinned by—she could see it now as she looked closer—a long, thin thorn. She reached up on tiptoe, her fingers just touching it.

She gripped the thorn and tugged. Kerauno gave a shrill whinny, like the shriek of a harpy, and tossed his head, jerking his wing away, folding it back up. The thorn slid free, causing Pippa to stumble back, right into . . . Ares! She quickly moved away from him, but the damage was done.

"What's going on here?" thundered the god.

He gazed, steely-eyed, at Bas, then at Pippa, and then at the thorn in Pippa's hand.

"What's this?" He reached over and took the thorn.

"It was stuck in Kerauno's wing," explained Pippa.

"A thorn?" said Ares, glaring at her. "Did you put it there?"

Pippa shook her head.

"She was helping me," Bas interjected. "Helping Kerauno. The thorn was causing him to fly off course. I don't know how it got there. Maybe while he was grazing?"

Ares ignored him. "Now is the time when tricks are played. An injured horse cannot race. A sly attempt, but foolish. Bas, come with me. At once! And you, girl, can take your tricks with you." He threw the thorn at Pippa's feet. Then he untied Kerauno's reins from the tree. "There, there, come," he told the monstrous horse, almost tenderly.

Bas glanced at Pippa apologetically as he walked away.

Pippa watched them go. She could feel anger at Ares bubbling up inside her.

Obviously it wasn't her fault. But it was someone's. Ares was right about one thing: there was no way the thorn had accidentally made its way into Kerauno's wing, not so deep and so purposefully placed. Someone had put it there, knowing Bas would struggle to remove it, if he even found it at all. Someone had wanted Kerauno not to race. But who?

* * *

Pippa had given up her search for the gods' palace. The thorn was all the three friends talked about that night at supper, huddled together on a bench in a corner of the courtyard.

Sophia examined it carefully. "It looks like a pomegranate thorn. But it is much larger than any I've ever seen. Someone is trying to sabotage you, Bas."

"It isn't fair," said Pippa. "Not even Kerauno deserves that. What did Ares say?"

Bas's voice grew thick. "He threatened my family again."

Pippa placed a hand on his shoulder.

"It must have been one of the riders," said Sophia. "Surely a god or goddess wouldn't have done it."

Pippa looked around the room. Everyone was busy eating or chatting. No one looked suspicious.

"Pomegranates do not grow on the mountain," said Sophia thoughtfully. "Of course, there is the myth . . ."

". . . of Persephone," finished Pippa.

It was her favorite tale of the gods, other than the stories of the winged horses, for it was a tale of family love, so unlike her own story. It told of a mother who truly loved her daughter and would do anything for her. Demeter's daughter, Persephone, was kidnapped by Hades, and Demeter missed her so much that when she mourned, her grief cast perpetual winter across the world.

At last, Hades had no choice but to give up Persephone, although he played a trick on the girl and convinced her to eat an enchanted pomegranate. When Persephone returned home, she still had the fruit, which she dropped upon seeing her mother. From it grew a pomegranate tree, unlike any other. It was said to mark an entrance to the Underworld. But only Hades knew its whereabouts. And perhaps his rider . . .

Pippa scanned the courtyard for Timon. But he wasn't there.

"Where's Timon?" she said.

Bas shrugged. "He never comes to meals."

"So what does he do instead of eat?" said Sophia.

"Practice?" said Pippa. She had seen him flying around the training course in the starlight, on her way back to the stables after supper. "He must really want to win. Enough to . . ."

"Enough to do this?" finished Bas, gesturing to the thorn. "If that's true, he's lucky Kerauno didn't kick him and snap him in two. I don't think he is strong enough to deal with my horse."

"We need to talk to Timon," said Sophia. "We need to find out more."

Bas and Pippa both agreed.

Pippa glanced again at the ominous thorn. Kerauno might be a monster. But no horse was born that way. Perhaps he had never known love. Without love to guide you, life was hard. No one knew this better than Pippa.

Aphrodite might have abandoned her, her parents too, but still she had Zeph. But for how long?

The last rays of the sun hung above them like the threads of the Fates, and she shivered.

Sixteen

Although they waited in the courtyard until long past supper, when all the food had been cleared away, Timon didn't arrive.

"Do you think he's in his room?" Bas wondered.

"Perhaps," said Sophia.

But Timon wasn't in his room either. In fact, it seemed as though he'd never been there at all. At first, Pippa stood near the door, hesitant to enter, but the room was so bare, it didn't feel like she was intruding.

There was no mosaic on the wall, no tub in the corner. No sandals lying out, or clothes, fresh or dirty. Just the bed, and even that looked like it had never been slept in, although Pippa had not used hers in a while either.

The only other item in the room was so small, she might have missed it had the moonlight not caught its edge. A silver coin, much like hers, half hidden under the bed. Pippa picked it up gently. Instead of a horse, the thin metal was stamped with the image of an anchor.

Sophia and Bas joined her, questioning looks upon their faces.

"An obolos," Sophia said as soon as she saw the coin. "The ferryman's fee, for entering the Underworld. But why would Timon have one?"

"I don't know," said Pippa. "But . . . I have one too."

She reached into the folds of her chiton and pulled out her coin, then handed both to Sophia.

"These aren't the same at all," replied Sophia, turning them over in her hands. "I'm not sure what yours is, but it's not an obolos."

Now, side by side, they did look different. Pippa's was larger, made of a thicker piece of silver. But if it wasn't an obolos, what was it?

"Besides, oboli are given to only those who are dead or dying," continued Sophia, handing the coin back to Pippa. "You wouldn't have been given one, nor would Timon. Unless . . ."

"Unless Timon is . . . dying . . . ," said Pippa slowly.

"He *looks* like he's dying," said Bas. "And he never eats."

"It doesn't make sense," said Sophia. "Surely Hades wants Timon to win, not *die*. Why would he choose a rider who's sick?"

"Who knows with Hades," said Bas. "Maybe the coin is for good luck?"

Sophia didn't seem convinced, but said, "We'll have to find Timon in the morning. It's getting late. Tomorrow is the last day before the race. We need our rest."

After placing the obolos back under Timon's bed, Sophia headed out of the room, with Bas close behind. Pippa, last to leave, glanced back and caught sight of the coin. It glinted again in the moonlight.

As Pippa walked back to the stables, her fingers played calmly, rhythmically, with her own coin. Inside her head, however, questions swirled. Why had her parents given her the coin, if it wasn't an obolos? Was it for good luck? But even if that was the case, why did it have a winged horse on it? And why had they left her in the first place? She had more questions now than ever.

She gazed up at the sky, as if it might have the answers. The moon was bright and round, almost like a coin itself.

And there, flying across its face, was the shadowy image of a horse. Once the horse had passed out of the shadows, Pippa could see a glint of golden hooves and shimmer of silver wings. Nikomedes. And on his back, a god so large it *had* to be Zeus. They were flying, up, up toward the stars and the constellation of Pegasus. Could it be that even the mightiest of gods missed his old steed?

Zeus gazed down at her for a moment, and she felt the urge to wave. But you didn't wave to a god.

You could wave to another rider though. In the distance, Pippa saw a second winged horse. Zeus wasn't the only one out riding after supper. So was Timon! They hadn't thought he would be out training in the dark, but he must be as determined to win as she was.

At least she could ask Timon about his coin. But to her surprise, Pippa watched him fly past the last flagpole—not around it—toward the setting sun.

Where was he headed?

Pippa didn't ponder for long. Instead, she ran to the

stables and swung up on to Zeph's back.

With a squeeze of her knees, they took off after him.

Already Timon was only a speck in the sky. Pippa urged Zeph on, and he seemed to understand the urgency, for he flew even faster.

Should she really be following Timon like this? *I'll find out where he's going, that's all*, thought Pippa.

Although the light was fading, Pippa was careful to keep her distance. Timon was flying neither up nor down but, it seemed, *around* the mountain. Would they end up back at the stables?

Before long they came to a meadow lit by the moon. Skotos swooped down and landed, and Pippa landed Zeph too, behind a row of boulders. She slipped off Zeph's back and peeked around the rocks.

The meadow was strangely barren except for a scattering of stones and a patch of golden narcissus. From the middle of these flowers grew an enormous tree, crooked and covered in red fruit. A pomegranate tree.

He did *do it*, thought Pippa. *Timon hurt Kerauno!*

This was surely enough proof. She should leave and return to the stables.

But she wanted to know more. Why did he have

an obolos? And where *was* he going? For he was still going, leading his steed past the tree and disappearing behind two large rocks on the other side of the field.

Pippa waited a few moments, then gestured to Zeph. "Come on. Let's follow." Zeph whinnied and stepped back.

"It's okay," said Pippa. "Come."

But Zeph whinnied again and refused. For a horse that loved new adventures, it was strange, but Pippa didn't want to force him. She remembered the taraxippoi and couldn't blame Zeph for being afraid.

"Wait here then, Zeph. I'll be back soon," she promised, and then headed across the meadow.

When she passed between the two boulders, she knew why Zeph wouldn't come.

There, like a gaping mouth, lay a hole in the earth, ringed with narcissus flowers, white as the moon. Obsidian stairs glimmered in the darkness, leading down, down, down. It was, without a doubt, the entrance to the Underworld.

And beside it was Timon, his horse waiting nearby.

The boy sat straight and still.

Pippa walked over and sat down beside him. "Timon?"

He blinked, surprised, as if not recognizing her for a moment.

"Timon?" she said again.

"Timotheos," he replied, at last. "That is my true name, if you must know. Hades changed my name when he brought me up here."

"*Up* here?" Pippa stammered, her heart beating fast. Suddenly everything made sense, why Timon never ate or slept. Why he could race for hours without rest. He wasn't just sick. . . .

"We were looking for you," she said, "Bas, Sophia, and me. I saw the coin under your bed."

"The coin," said Timon. "I must have dropped it."

"It's an obolos. Does that mean you're . . ."

"Yes. I am dead. I have been brought up from the Underworld to race."

Pippa gasped. "Surely Hades can't do that! Why would he? I don't understand."

The boy's dark eyes shimmered.

"Hades can do what he wishes. Besides, it's not his fault. I begged him to pick me. I always wanted to race. But I died before I was chosen."

How? Pippa wondered, but did not ask. He was so young.

"I thought this could be my chance to change my fate." He smiled sadly. "But some fates you can't change."

A fire sparked inside Pippa.

"Are you sure, Timon?" she asked, thinking of her coin and what she had discovered about it, and added, "Maybe some things can change. Maybe this is your chance."

He shook his head. "I don't belong here. I knew it the moment we woke up in the courtyard."

"I felt that way too, at first," said Pippa. "But Bellerophon was right, we're all riders here."

Timon shook his head again. "I just want to go home, to the Underworld."

"Then why don't you?" Pippa pointed to the entrance. "It's right there."

"I can't," said Timon. "I can only return if I train as hard as I am able and then race. It was part of my arrangement with Hades. So for now, I wait. Why were you looking for me?"

"I . . . ," began Pippa, but then, between the boulders, she saw something move in the field.

Another boy, with another horse, lurking under the pomegranate tree.

Seventeen

It was difficult for Pippa to make out who it was.

She jumped up, expecting Timon to do the same, but he remained seated, lost in thought, staring down at the entrance he couldn't go through.

So as much as Pippa wanted to ask him more about his coin and the Underworld, and possibly even her parents, she left Timon and made her way through the boulders, into the meadow.

As she neared the boy by the tree, she could finally see who it was. His sharp chin was unmistakable. Khrys. His horse, Khruse, stood nearby.

Khrys was holding a small woolen bag, into which he was stuffing a twig from the tree. It protruded from the bag, gnarled and thorny.

"Stop!" Pippa cried.

Khrys looked up. His eyes narrowed.

"You!" he spat. "What are *you* doing here?" He shook the bag at her, and the twig shook too, like an accusatory finger.

"I could ask you the same," replied Pippa. "But I already know. You've been picking thorns and using them to hurt the horses."

"Horses?" Khrys shook his head. "Only *one* horse—so far. And you should be grateful."

"It's wrong to hurt a horse—any horse," cried Pippa. "You're cheating! Just wait until I tell Bellerophon."

Pippa expected Khrys to drop the bag and beg her to reconsider, but instead, he laughed. "Ha! Go ahead. I'm not the only one. Haven't you realized that by now?"

Pippa didn't want to believe it, but perhaps he was right. Timon, being from the Underworld, was impossibly light. Skotos wouldn't even feel him on his back. Ares wanted Bas to do whatever it took to win and had even given him a spear, though she knew Bas would never use it. "Even Theodoros, with the food . . . ,"

Pippa murmured aloud, remembering how she'd see the nymphs feeding his horse special seagrass. Sophia still seemed determined to win by skill alone. And her, of course.

"Good for Theodoros!" Khrys's eyes glittered.

"But you *can't* hurt a horse. It's cruel. Bellerophon won't like it!"

"Tell him then. What's he going to do? He's not a god or goddess. Maybe if you told Aphrodite. But from what I hear, she never visits you. She didn't even *pick* you. You were that pathetic horse's choice."

An image flashed into Pippa's mind. A horse leaning over her and a goddess saying to him, "If you wish, little one." Maybe her dream had been real.

Khrys sneered. "Why don't you just go home? Oh, right. You can't. You don't have a home to go to, *foundling.*" His words seared like the sun's rays. "*I* grew up with chariot *winners*; I know what it takes to win, but you don't. And when you're gone, your horse will be nothing but horse meat."

"No!" said Pippa. "I have to win!"

Khrys threw down the bag. "You'll be needing this, then."

And with that, Apollo's rider leaped onto his horse

and took off into the night.

The bag lay at Pippa's feet.

A white muzzle poked around from behind her and sniffed the bag. Zeph. When had he joined her? She turned into him, burrowing into the crook of his neck, taking deep breaths of his earthy, sweet-hay smell. But it didn't calm her as it usually did.

Zeph nudged her with his nose, and she looked up at him, blinking back tears. She had to save Zeph—if she didn't do something, he would be . . . Khrys was right. But . . .

"I can't hurt a horse," she sobbed. "I'm not like Khrys. . . ." But who was she then? Like Timon? No, she'd been training. She would not give in to her fate.

Still, she did not reach for the bag of thorns. She left it there in the field and slipped onto Zeph's back.

The map led her back to the stables. All the way, Pippa's heart hammered with hurt and anger, and she was so lost in her feelings that she didn't see the hunched figure in Zeph's stall until she almost collided with it.

"Watch it!" came a crackly voice.

Zeph landed, and Pippa practically fell off him at the sight of the woman, so gnarled she looked like the root of a tree. It was the Fate Atropos.

Her shears were stuck in a loop of her linen belt, and she was wearing a cloak that covered her grizzled hair. Pippa had only seen her sitting down before. Standing up, she was not much taller.

"Don't you know how to land that creature by now?" snapped Atropos.

"What are you doing here?" asked Pippa, climbing down from Zeph's back.

"What *am* I doing here," grouched the Fate, rolling her eyes.

"I thought you didn't want anything to do with the races?"

"I don't. We shouldn't be part of this foolery, if you ask me. This is Aphrodite's job, and if she doesn't care whether you have a costume, well, so be it!" She waved her gnarled hand in the air. "But my sisters insisted you must race. Love must have its chance. And, of course, I drew the shortest thread. Just my luck."

"You brought my costume?" Pippa's eyes caught sight of it, folded in the hay just behind the old woman. "So . . . I'll win, after all? My training . . . it has changed things?"

But the Fate's answer came quickly, like a dreadful

snip. "Of course not," she said, and stepped out into the hallway. Then, like a crease smoothed away into nothingness, she was gone.

"Wait!" Pippa rushed out of the stall. Only darkness spread out as far as she could see.

Pippa's hand trembled as she closed the gate, returning to Zeph . . . and her costume.

In the hay by the manger lay her outfit for the race. A new chiton, folded neatly, glimmering with golden roses. But it was the helmet that angered her.

It was a full face mask that disguised the wearer's identity. The type of fancy helmet men wore in elite displays of military horsemanship, made of bronze with a thin leather strap that fastened behind the head. A winged horse feather, clearly one of Zeph's, rose from the top with a flourish. But the face on the helmet wasn't a horse's—or even a human's. Although Pippa had not yet seen her, no other face could be as beautiful as this. It was Aphrodite's, smiling up at her.

Pippa glared back.

Once again, the goddess had avoided her. The other gods and goddesses had given their costumes to their riders in person. But not Aphrodite. She too had given up on Pippa. She hadn't even sent one of her Graces.

Maybe if she had helped me, I would have a chance. Only the Fates care if I race—to make sure their prediction comes true.

Pippa had done everything she could. If they weren't going to win, it was because no one believed in her. Except—*she* believed! And Zeph did too. He'd chosen her, after all.

Pippa didn't want to wear Aphrodite's face during the race. She'd rather wear Ares's. At least then she'd be wearing the face of a winner.

That was it! Suddenly, she had an idea.

Pippa hugged Zeph hard.

Maybe she *didn't* have to wear the helmet. Maybe she could wear something else, *be* someone else.

Maybe she *could* change her fate, after all.

Eighteen

The next day, the day before the race, the riders woke to find brightly colored clouds circling the top of Mount Olympus like crowns. "Zeus has put them there," announced Bellerophon at breakfast. "They mark tomorrow's course."

His announcement was followed by a flurry of gods and goddesses coming and going, much to his annoyance, with pearls that needed to be braided into manes, last-minute advice for the race, and a hundred other things besides. There was not a moment for Pippa to tell Sophia and Bas anything about the night before.

Dionysus appeared at lunch, drinking cup after cup of wine; Hephaestus was caught trying to inscribe his name on the lightning bolt statue; and Artemis led a hunt through the training course, which sent Bellerophon into a rage. He banned all gods and goddesses from making further appearances until the next morning, at the start of the race.

But then, as Pippa and the rest of the riders were leading their horses past the stables to the grazing fields, they saw a terrible sight. Water was streaming from the stalls and down the side of the mountain, carrying hay and buckets and even reins and saddlecloths along with it. The air smelled salty, like the sea.

From one of the stalls, on a wave of water, burst Poseidon. His hair and beard whipped in whirlpools, and his eyes stormed. He landed in front of the stables in a frothing pool.

"*Poseidon!* How dare you?" raged Bellerophon, splashing up to him.

"How *dare* I? How *dare* you!"

"It wasn't me. It was your brother!" said Bellerophon.

"So *Zeus* sent home *my* rider? He disqualified *my* horse from the race? *Me*, god of the sea, patron of horses! This would never have happened if I was allowed to race my hippocampi!"

Now that Pippa thought about it, Theodoros had been absent since lunch. And his horse, the stallion with the sky-blue wings, was gone too. So he had been disqualified. Zeus must have found out about the sea-weed.

"I warned you!" Bellerophon shouted back, pounding his cane on the ground. He turned to the riders.

"Take your horses to graze," he yelled. "Leave this mess to me."

"But Theodoros . . . ?" stammered Pippa.

"He will not be coming back."

The grass in the pasture looked indigo in the twilight. Even the sun seemed to have been drenched in Poseidon's rage. All the riders stood quietly, watching their horses graze. Some children whispered that Theodoros hadn't only been sent home, he had been sent home as a fish. But Bellerophon hadn't mentioned that, so no one was sure.

"Imagine, after all that—not racing," Sophia said to Bas and Pippa. "How ashamed Theodoros's family will be." She shook her head. "As much as we have our differences, I would still like to make my father proud. I wish he could see me tomorrow."

"And see you lose?" Khrys taunted, striding over, followed closely by Perikles. "No mortals get to watch the races. But the Oracle will learn the results from the gods, and my father will be with her when she does. My father is having a private audience with her all day."

Sophia rolled her eyes.

"I thought you said the only reason he's doing that is so that he's the first one to know if you embarrassed him," said Perikles. "Like that time—"

"Hush!" said Khrys, his face turning red. "I said no such thing. Come on. It is nearly time for supper." He stormed off, with Perikles trailing behind, looking confused.

"Good riddance," muttered Sophia. "Even Khrys's own family doesn't like him. I'm not surprised."

Bas remained silent.

Pippa fingered her coin. If her parents could see her now, would they be proud?

It didn't matter. . . . What mattered was her plan.

Now, with all the gods and goddesses gone, and Khrys too, she could tell it at last to her friends. She gathered them in a quiet spot of the pasture and started with all that had happened the night before.

"Timon is from the Underworld?!" Bas's eyes went wide, and he flicked his gaze to the slight boy, who was standing away from the others, watching Skotos eat.

"Not so surprising perhaps," said Sophia. "Neither is the news about Khrys's cheating. I should have guessed it. I wish I had been there to give him a piece of my mind."

But both Sophia and Bas were surprised when, in a whisper, Pippa told them her idea. "It was the riding outfits that gave me the idea. The masks will hide our faces. Kerauno's been the sure winner from the start. As long as his rider doesn't fall off. Don't you see?"

Bas and Sophia shook their heads.

"Bas and I can switch horses!"

"Oh!" breathed Bas. "If I ride Zeph, I'll lose and get to go home. If you ride Kerauno you'll win, and then you'll get to be . . ."

". . . with Zeph forever," said Pippa. "Exactly."

Exactly right and exactly wrong at the same time.

Pippa pushed the feeling aside. If she wanted to stay with Zeph, if she wanted to keep him safe, it was the only way.

Bas's eyes were bright with hope. "It's perfect.

Perfect, Pippa. Ares doesn't care who's riding. As long as his horse wins, he'll be happy. And Aphrodite? She hasn't even bothered to meet Pippa, so I can't see her minding, either."

"Didn't you hear what happened to Theodoros?" Sophia cried, a little too loudly.

"But this is different," said Pippa in a rush, wishing for a moment she had only told Bas. "We aren't really cheating. We're just . . . *switching*."

Sophia shook her head, but she said, "I suppose. Though I have never heard of such a thing happening in a race."

"But that doesn't mean we can't," said Pippa forcefully. "Please, I have to do *something*."

Sophia frowned. "Riding your best *is* doing something."

"Riding my best won't help me win," said Pippa. "The Fates told me so."

"You met the *Fates*?" Sophia's eyes widened.

"By accident," said Pippa, explaining her visit, and Atropos's second appearance. She ended by showing Sophia and Bas the map.

"No wonder you can fly around the mountain without getting lost," said Bas. Then added, "I don't understand it. Why would it be fated that you must lose?"

"It doesn't matter," said Pippa. "*We* are going to change it."

After a long pause, Sophia said, "While I don't think you should try to trick the gods and goddesses, you and Bas should do what you must. I am still going to ride my hardest."

"Of course," said Pippa.

"But it is a clever plan," she added.

Pippa smiled. Coming from Sophia, that was high praise.

Sophia reached for Pippa's hand. "Nikepteros."

"Nikepteros," Pippa murmured back, giving Sophia's hand a squeeze. *Victory in flight.*

Later though, as Pippa got Zeph ready for the next morning, she wondered whether her plan really *was* so clever. She hated that she was taking advice from Khrys. But it was not the same as hurting a horse, and that made her feel better.

All that really mattered was Zeph. "When I win, I will stay in these stables and care for you," she whispered in the horse's ear. Yes, Ares would be Zeus for a day . . . but it was just a day, not forever, and she would make sure Zeph was safe. She reached for his brush. "Kerauno can live with Zeus and carry the thunderbolts. You'd rather chase butterflies, wouldn't you?" She gave him a playful kiss on the nose, then began to comb his coat, brushing until it shone.

When she was finished, she braided the pearls into his mane one by one. They looked like sunlight glinting off the water. Pippa hugged Zeph tight, knowing it might be the last time she was with him, alone, until after the race.

"It's okay," she said. "At least, soon it will be. Trust me."

Zeph snorted. Was he disagreeing with her? She should have known he wouldn't like the plan. Horses did not like secrets.

Nineteen

The day of the race dawned clear and bright. The only clouds were the colorful ones that ringed the mountain and marked the course. But Pippa knew the good weather wouldn't last. Bellerophon had warned them that Zeus always conjured foul weather during a race to further challenge the riders. What would it be this time? A hurricane? A snowstorm? Fog, like those three children—now taraxippoi—had been lost in?

A hush fell over the stables as the riders readied themselves and their horses.

Pippa slipped the golden bridle on Zeph, and he waited impatiently, nudging her as she changed into her clothes for the race. She had avoided her chambers in the chance, unlikely as it may be, that Pandaisia, the Grace, was there to dress her. Her outfit, after all, was far from standard. Besides the special chiton Atropos had brought for her, she was wearing a large cloak from her room. That had been Sophia's brilliant suggestion.

Bas was going to wear his cloak, too. The cloaks, tucked around them, would help disguise their different sizes. But would that be enough? She didn't know. She touched the coin she'd hidden in the folds of her chiton, under the cloak, and thought of her parents— and hoped Bas would soon be reunited with his.

Khrys passed by and scoffed at her. "A cloak like that will only weigh you down."

But he said no more, for there was a loud whistle. "It is time! Riders, come!" called Bellerophon from outside.

Khrys hurried away.

The stomp of hooves and beating of wings filled the stables as the riders and horses left. Pippa held her breath, listening.

When all was quiet, Bas stepped into Zeph's stall. "Here," he said, and handed Pippa his helmet. She gave him hers.

While Aphrodite's mask was beautiful, this one, with Ares's face on it, was stern and ruthless. And heavier too.

Another whistle split the air.

"Go," urged Bas.

Pippa gave Zeph one final hug and felt the pearls studding his mane press into her cheek. His muscles tensed, as though he knew something was wrong.

"I'll be with you soon," Pippa whispered.

Then, she put on the helmet, and before Zeph could see her, slipped into Kerauno's stall and mounted the monster.

The riders, led by Bellerophon on his own steed, flew past the golden columns and storied colonnades of the palace, up, up to the highest peak, where the race would begin. The gods and goddesses, as well as winners of past races, were already gathered there.

Their seats were like steps, carved into the mountainside in a semicircle, much like the seats in the hippodrome in Athens, which were dug into the hillside. But this was no hill. Instead of looking out onto a racetrack, the seats looked out onto the sky. There was only a small stone outcropping, like a ledge, directly below for the horses to start from. Bellerophon landed there and directed the riders to follow.

As Pippa and the others swooped in and took their places in a row, the gods and goddesses began to cheer, stomping and clapping wildly. Pippa could feel the ledge shake.

She struggled to see through the eyeholes of the heavy helmet. It was much too big and fitted badly. Kerauno jostled under her, flexing his wings. But he was calm compared to Zeph. Pippa saw him, further down the line, tossing his head, trying to jerk the reins away from Bas, searching for her. Pippa wanted to go to him and soothe away his fear. *Soon enough*, she thought.

She looked behind her, up at the crowd in the stands. All the seats were full. Besides a great gathering of gods and goddesses—the only one noticeably absent was Poseidon— there were also the Muses, the Graces, nymphs, and dryads . . . It seemed everyone from Mount Olympus had gathered to watch the race. There were even centaurs, which made sense to Pippa, since

they were half human, half horse. Pippa tried to spot
Aphrodite among the crowd, but found Ares instead,
high in the stands, standing with his arms crossed.

How would he feel if he knew that it was not his
rider wearing his helmet right now but Pippa? Thank
the Muses that he was too distracted to notice.

He was arguing with a goddess who Pippa couldn't
make out. Could it be Aphrodite? But before she could
adjust the helmet to get a better look, there was the
sound of a whistle.

"Behold!" cried Bellerophon. "The god of the sky.
The king of the gods! The judge of the race!"

All heads turned, including Pippa's, toward a swirl-
ing cloud, high above.

Out of the cloud emerged a silver wing. The very
same wing Pippa had seen so many weeks ago now, in
the storm in Athens.

"And behold his steed, Nikomedes!" announced
Bellerophon.

The horse swooped down out of the cloud, his
golden hooves glittering. On his back was Zeus, twice
as tall as any of the other gods, with a beard so big
it obscured his face, and so frizzled it seemed to have
been struck by lightning. Both horse and god tossed

their heads, as they swooped through the sky. Their sleek muscles flexed and shone in the sunlight.

"Huzzah!" the god of gods cried as Nikomedes landed on a floating platform, in front of everyone. A beautiful mountain nymph was on it to greet him, along with a boy wearing a golden crown. Pippa could just make him out. It was Dion, the winner of the last race so many years ago. The boy bowed to Zeus, removed the crown, and handed it to him. Zeus raised it up and waved it at the riders.

Pippa's hands were sweating now, and her hair, under the helmet, was matted to her forehead. Kerauno jostled beneath her, and it took all her effort to keep him from lowering his head. As long as she kept his head back, he could not buck. As much as she hated to be rough with a horse, it was the only way to keep Kerauno in control. Her knees, scissored to his sides, already ached.

"The time has come," said Bellerophon. Although his voice was loud, there was a quaver in it. Was he nervous, too? "My thanks once more goes to Echo"— he waved to the mountain nymph positioned beside Zeus—"who shall again be the orator of this great race. But let me first remind all of you of the rules. Three times you race around the mountaintop. No harming each other's steeds in any way. The first horse and rider to cross this mark—"

"Oh, enough already!" Zeus boomed. "LET THE RACE BEGIN!"

Twenty

With a great *crack*, a lightning bolt blazed through the sky. For a moment, all the horses and riders, Pippa included, remained frozen, until Bellerophon cried, "Go! *Go!*"

The horses lunged forward. And Kerauno was fastest. He shot off the mountain like an arrow, and it was all Pippa could do to hang on. Bas's helmet rocked back and forth on her head as they took the lead, so she wasn't sure if it was her imagination or real, the voice that rang out, "And they're off, off, off!"

She couldn't listen; she had to concentrate, to stay on Kerauno. It took all her strength to hold the reins tight to his neck and keep her legs clenched to his sides. The voice faded, lost in the mighty draft from the beast's wings.

Kerauno tried to throw her more than once, but she managed to stay on. Her legs throbbed, her arms too, as they sped on, like a hurricane, to the far side of the mountaintop.

Only clouds lay ahead of them, and behind them, the spectators had disappeared from view. The rocks below were sharp and craggy, like the teeth of a manticore.

Except . . . Were those three old women she saw, sitting together on the rocks, waving flags? Were they the Fates? Pippa glanced back for another look, but the helmet blocked her view. She tried again, and though she did not see the old women, she glimpsed the horses behind her: Khrys on Khruse, Timon on Skotos, and behind them, Sophia on Ajax. She couldn't see Bas and Zeph.

Soon Pippa and Kerauno were rounding the mountain, approaching the stands again, and the sounds of cheering and singing greeted them: "'Aloft wings beat and feathers fly, hark the horses of the sky!'"

The chant grew louder as the crowd came back into sight. "HARK THE HORSES OF THE SKY!"

"Kerauno remains in the lead, lead, lead!" cried the mythic maiden Echo, living up to her name. "Set to win, win, win."

The words filled Pippa with fire, and seemingly Kerauno too, for he flew even faster as he began his second lap. The clouds ahead were still wispy and white. Perhaps Zeus was not intending to play with the weather. Perhaps her plan would work, now that she had Kerauno under control. As she neared the spot she thought she'd seen the Fates, she looked for them, a feeling of self-satisfaction growing in her chest. She'd show them . . .

Whish! Snap!

Kerauno reared up without warning. Pippa slipped, and for a moment, she was airborne, connected to the horse only by her grip on his reins. Then *thud!* She landed back on the golden saddlecloth and struggled to regain her focus. She looked over her shoulder to try to see her attacker. It was Khrys, a whip in his hand.

"Stop!" cried Pippa, not thinking to disguise her voice.

"Pippa!" came Khrys's reply. He sounded both disgusted and impressed.

Snap! He cracked the whip again.

This time it struck Kerauno, and he reared straight up, then lurched back down and began to buck. The reins jerked from Pippa's hands, and she was tossed off Kerauno's back, onto the horse's wing.

Bas's helmet covered her eyes; she could see nothing. The cape tangled around her body. She could hardly move.

Pippa clutched blindly at the feathers but couldn't grab hold. Kerauno was beating his wings furiously, trying to shake her off.

She felt herself slip . . .

Twenty-one

Whoosh! Thump! Just as Pippa began to fall, something collided with Kerauno's side, startling the horse nearly into stillness.

The collision jostled Pippa back into place, where she groped desperately for something to hold on to. Her fingers curled around a handful of mane, and a moment later, she was grasping the reins.

Pulling herself back up, she untangled the cape, straightened the helmet, and was able to see again.

There, beside her, was a thin black steed. Timon's horse. Although Skotos did not look hurt, the horse's back was bare, and the reins hung free. Timon was gone!

"Timon!" she cried, and fearfully looked down. She caught a glimpse of something, but clouds obscured her view.

Timon had held back and swerved his horse into hers. He'd saved her, and fallen because of it.

Of course, Timon could not be hurt, but what had happened to him? She hoped with all her heart that he would make it back to the Underworld, back where he felt he belonged.

Around her, the wind wailed. Zeus was brewing a storm, after all. In the distance, black clouds rolled in, engulfing the riders ahead of her. *Most* of them were ahead of her now, including Khrys.

Pippa had to make up the lost time. The third lap was approaching, and the sound of the crowd, no longer singing now but shouting, once again filled the air.

"Aho! A new horse has taken the lead! Khruse soars ahead, Ajax follows, as the third and final lap begins! Feathers fly, fly, fly . . . And lightning too!"

Lightning *was* zigging and zagging in front of Pippa. It crackled and buzzed, illuminating the sky in

bursts of brightness.

Pippa crouched low, raised up slightly above Kerauno's back, as she directed the horse around the flashes. Rain fell, battering against her helmet. The cloak, untucked and flapping behind her now, was torn away by a blast of wind.

The storm did not slow Kerauno. Pippa leaned into him as he overtook the other horses one by one, including Zeph. She could see Bas struggling to keep her little horse on course. *Is he looking for me?* she wondered. She didn't know, but turned her attention back to the race. At last, she caught up with Khrys. He too was focused.

The clouds tumbled and heaved in front of them. A flash lit up the sky, and Kerauno roared. Khrys turned his head and caught sight of her, his focus broken, his eyes wide in surprise. Pippa saw his hand reach back—for his whip?—when a second bolt of lightning split the sky. Pippa managed to maneuver Kerauno out of its path. But it struck Khrys and, with a flash and a cry, horse and rider spun down in a flurry of golden feathers.

The helmet had shifted again, and Pippa couldn't see. Enough! The cloak was gone, anyway. Her disguise was useless. She knocked off the helmet, and it tumbled down, down to the stones below.

Pippa could see now. Khruse was still in the air, though just barely, with Khrys clinging to his back. They were all right. But they were far off course and would never regain their position.

Pippa was in the lead now. Only half a lap of the mountain to go. Everyone would see she wasn't Bas, but she didn't care. It was almost all over.

A row of clouds that wasn't there before stretched out in front of her. The finish line. The crowd was cursing and roaring now. Echo cried, "Faster than anyone thought possible, here he flies, flies, flies."

Pippa was sure she had won. And Echo hadn't noticed the switch. But then Pippa saw something out of the corner of her eye, a small white shape she'd know anywhere. Zeph!

The orator *wasn't* talking about Kerauno. She was talking about Zeph!

The little horse was almost neck and neck with them now. Pippa glanced over at him. He looked magnificent. Never had she seen him so concentrated, so focused—on *her*!

Pippa urged Kerauno on. She needed to win. For

Zeph's sake. Faster, faster went Kerauno. And Zeph kept pace.

Crack! Lightning lit the sky. Kerauno flinched, and Pippa was momentarily blinded. When she could see again, there was Zeph, out in front. The line of clouds marking the finish was gone.

The race was over.

Zeph had won!

Twenty-two

Pippa was dazed. As the lightning storm stopped as quickly as it had started, a new storm—a storm of feelings—swirled inside her. Zeph—*her* Zeph—had won! He had proved them all wrong. He had flown the fastest!

But *she* had lost.

She circled Kerauno down and landed on the outcropping where Bellerophon was standing. The great groom's eyes were wide with disbelief.

Bas was already there with Zeph, his mask off, a look of horror upon his face.

"We won?" Bas sounded incredulous.

"*You* won?" snorted Sophia, joining them with Ajax.

"Zeph!" shouted Pippa. She slid off Kerauno's back and ran to the little horse, kissing his nose and sputtering in the same breath. "I knew you could do it! But, oh, oh, what have you done?"

Zeph didn't seem to care, only wanting to nuzzle with Pippa.

Pippa cradled Zeph's head and stroked his nose, as the other riders landed behind her. "I should have trusted you."

Bellerophon strode over, his cane pounding the ground with each step. "There are a hundred rules and a hundred ways to break them. But this?! I've never seen this!"

"I . . . I thought it was the only way," stammered Pippa. "The Fates—"

"I told you not to listen to them!" The great groom cursed. "You'll be punished. You have to be! The race needs rules! You think you can choose a horse better than the gods? Why, you might as well have flown to their palace and seated yourself on a throne!"

"Isn't that what you tried to . . . ," started Pippa.

Bellerophon blinked. He pounded the ground again with his cane but said nothing.

"And there was lots of rule breaking," continued Pippa. "Everyone was . . ."

"Everyone was *not* switching horses," stormed Bellerophon, finding his tongue.

"Ares will be furious," cried Bas, in a panic. "If Kerauno had won, even with you on his back, Pippa, that would have meant Ares had won. He wouldn't have cared that it wasn't me riding. But now . . ."

Bas was right.

"Foul! *Foul!*" Ares had left the stands and was now on the ledge, shaking his spear in the air. His face was red, his hair wet from the storm. "That's my rider, but that's *not* my horse."

"And that's my horse, but not my rider," called out a woman's voice. Behind Ares strode a goddess.

She was wearing a long chiton that was neither dyed nor decorated, and her hair fell down her back in wet tangles. No black kohl emphasized her eyes or exaggerated her eyebrows. No beetroot flushed her cheeks or lips. She was not wearing rings or mulberry clusters in her ears. Her mask had made her out to be prettier. She was surprisingly plain. If it wasn't for the rose decorating her fan, and the fact she stood taller than any mortal, Pippa might not have known it was her, the goddess of love.

"This is not what I expected," said Aphrodite. Her face was twisted with emotion, and Pippa could not tell if the goddess was about to cry or laugh.

Ares pointed his spear at the great groom. "Bellerophon, were you not overseeing our riders?! How did you let such a thing occur?!"

Bellerophon pulled at his hair. He looked unsure of what to say, afraid of the god's great wrath.

"If these children have bent the rules, don't blame him," said Aphrodite.

"Then I shall blame *you!*" cried Ares. He swung his arm and flung his spear. From it burst more spears that shot through the air toward the goddess.

With a grand sweep of her fan, Aphrodite conjured a wall of roses that climbed from earth to air, blocking the spears. They fell to the ground with a clatter.

"SILENCE!" ordered Zeus. He leaped from the platform down to the ledge, landing so hard it seemed like the rocky outcrop might crumble away.

"Why are you two fighting again?! What in mortal's mayhem is going on?!"

Despite the rain, his beard was still as big as a tree-top. His eyes sparked like lightning.

Fear coursed through Pippa as she gazed up at the mighty god.

She should have listened to Sophia. What was going to happen now? Zeus was angry—furious—at Ares and Aphrodite most of all, it seemed, but that didn't mean he wouldn't exact his wrath on them, the mortals. There were plenty of examples of that. Zeus could do anything. Make them endlessly roll a stone up a mountain—or even turn them *to* stone!

Riders and horses, gods and goddesses, nymphs and dryads alike grew silent and still. Even the mountain itself was quiet.

"Tell us what happened here," Zeus demanded, shaking the golden crown. Pippa could see now that it was made of three interwoven golden feathers. "Who is to blame? Who must be punished?"

Ares opened his mouth, but Zeus hushed him. "Not you! I've heard enough from *you*. The mortals. What have you to say for yourselves?"

Pippa could see Bas was near tears.

"It's my fault!" she burst out.

"Really?" said Zeus, his eyebrows rising.

"Let me explain . . . ," she started, but her voice stuck in her throat. She looked up at Zeus. His eyebrows were relaxed now. And the flash of lightning in his eye seemed more like a twinkle. She saw him glance up at the sky, then touch a feather pinned to his robes. It was a winged horse feather, but bright as a star. Was it from Pegasus, his first horse? Zeus must have been going to visit Pegasus when she saw him flying the other night. Maybe the feather was a way to remember the steed, when Zeus had to tend to business on Mount Olympus. He must really love Pegasus, just like she loved Zeph.

And that gave Pippa hope and courage. Maybe Zeus, all-powerful as he was, would understand.

"Let . . . let me explain" Pippa started again. "We switched horses. Bas didn't want to win. He wants to go home. I love Zeph—Zephyr. I want to stay here with him. So I thought that if we switched horses, I would win on Kerauno and he would lose on Zeph."

"But how then did Zephyr win?" asked Zeus.

They all looked at Zeph, who was nuzzling Pippa's hand. She shook her head. "I don't know. Maybe it was the lightning . . ."

"It was love," said Aphrodite emphatically. "Don't

you see? Zephyr saw Pippa and flew to be by her side. Love should be rewarded. Besides, it is my horse that won, is it not? The right thing to do is for Zephyr to win and to allow Hippolyta to stay with him here."

Ares stomped his foot. "But that mortal *didn't* win! You can't reward her. Or that pathetic creature!"

"Zeus won't choose war over love," snapped Aphrodite.

A look of frustration passed over Zeus's face. "Can't? Won't? How dare you presume! I choose what I wish."

Zeph snorted. His ears were turned back. Pippa could tell he didn't like the arguing. "Shhh," she murmured, her own breath tight.

Zeus stared piercingly at both of them. "Love, hmm . . . ," he muttered, stroking his beard.

Pippa's hand went in her chiton, reaching for her coin. *Please*, she thought. *Please. . . .*

"I choose"—the king of the gods paused dramatically—"neither! Send the two mortals back to Earth—at once!"

"So we *both* lose?" cried Ares.

"Hush, Ares . . . ," started Aphrodite.

"This is all *your* fault!" The two began, once again, to argue.

Bas looked elated, but Pippa felt as if Zeus *had* actually turned her to stone. But this was worse. She would never see Zeph again. She threw her arms around his neck, burying her face in his mane. She couldn't leave him. Not after everything. She looked over defiantly at Zeus, whose attention was on the arguing pair.

"No!" she said.

"No?" Zeus boomed. He looked away from Ares and Aphrodite, and glared at Pippa. His eyes flashed red.

What have I done? thought Pippa. She clutched Zeph's neck.

"You *dare* challenge me? For a horse?"

"Yes," said Pippa, barely believing the words coming out of her mouth. "For a horse. For Zeph."

Zeus looked like he was about to say something, but instead he touched his feather again, and his expression softened. He gave Aphrodite a nod. "Now *that* is love. You may be a mortal, but you have a mighty heart. Bah," he sighed. "Take the horses with you. I've had enough of troublemakers for more than a mortal's lifetime!"

Ares groaned with displeasure. But Pippa's heart swelled.

Had Zeus really just banished Zeph with her? As he waved his hand to enforce his decree, Kerauno reared up.

With a sharp screeching whinny, like the sound of a thousand dying crows, the black horse lurched into the air and sped off into the sky.

Zeus sighed again and rubbed his temples. "So be it! Let that one banish himself. Come, riders, it is time to feast. Not *you*," he said to Bas and Pippa. He glanced at Aphrodite. "Take them away."

"But someone needs to win!" roared Ares.

Zeus paused. "I do need a new horse to carry my lightning bolts," he said. "Very well. The first two places are disqualified. The winner of the race is Athena's horse, Ajax. Zeus has spoken!"

Ares cried out in rage and stormed off.

Pippa looked over at Sophia, still astride Ajax, who stood so proudly he almost glowed. Was Sophia proud, too? It had not been a clear victory. But Sophia's grin told Pippa how happy she was. After all, she had chosen not to cheat. She and Ajax had won fairly.

Pippa smiled.

"Goodbye, Sophia," she whispered.

Sophia smiled back. "Farewell," she mouthed.

Aphrodite took Zeph's reins and gestured to Pippa and Bas to follow. "Come. Come with me. Quickly, before he changes his mind."

Pippa would miss the feast and the grand celebration, when Nikomedes flew into the sky and became a constellation near Pegasus. She'd miss Ajax taking his place by Zeus's side. Most of all, though, she'd miss Sophia. But no one deserved to win more than she and Ajax, both honorable and wise, and her friends, besides.

Twenty-three

The mountainside was wet from the rain. Trees dripped and rocks glistened as Aphrodite led them down. Bas walked on ahead, a bounce in his step, obviously excited to be heading home, while Zeph flew near Pippa and the goddess, skimming the ground. Once, Pippa had so many questions to ask the goddess, but now she didn't know what to say.

"Zeus can change his mind like the weather," said Aphrodite. Unlike the Grace who'd spoken in musical tones, Aphrodite's voice was ordinary. "I would have liked to win, of course, but this is a good outcome for you."

Pippa wasn't sure. She had no home to return to. How could she keep Zeph? And how would a winged horse live outside of Olympus? Bellerophon had said they couldn't exist. What did that mean? He would never let harm come to one of his horses, would he?

Pippa's worry grew with every step she took until it could grow no more and burst out as anger. She glared at Aphrodite and scolded, "You never came to see me. You never brought me gifts. I had no one to ask what to do. I had to make all my own decisions."

"When I went down to the mortal realm," Aphrodite said slowly, "I was planning on choosing your master's son."

"So I *was* a mistake . . ." Pippa felt her anger growing.

Aphrodite shook her head and remained calm. "Zeph, however, had other plans," she continued. "He pulled me away from the stables, toward you. I wanted to let something grow out of love. Not force a match with might. That's why I didn't meddle, like all the other gods would have. I knew you had Zeph. I trusted you, Hippolyta, to do the right things. True love is trusting. *Completely.*"

There was a long pause, as the words settled in the air. Pippa wasn't so sure, but . . . "Do you think I should have trusted Zeph?" she whispered.

"Perhaps," said Aphrodite, with a nod. But then she added, "Had you not been ahead of him, would he have flown to catch up? Who is to know?"

"The Fates. They knew all along," thought Pippa aloud. "Oh . . ." She pulled out the map of Mount Olympus from beneath her chiton. "This belongs to them. I promised I would leave it behind."

She handed the map to Aphrodite, who looked surprised. "A gift from the Fates. That is rare. See, Hippolyta, you found your own gifts. Your own way." She handed it back. "You may still need it."

"They told me I would lose." Pippa went on, "Did they know Zeph would win? Did they know all along?"

"Don't give the Fates too much credit, my dear," laughed the goddess. "They are merely three old ladies, and even they can only see so much."

Pippa glared at her. She didn't want to be so easily enraptured by this goddess, who seemed both nice and knowing. "If you know so much, what is this? Why was I left with it?" She pulled the coin out. "Does it have something to do with my parents?"

Aphrodite looked at it. "I am not sure, other than it is a sign that you were loved—and love horses."

"I was not loved," insisted Pippa, anger welling in her. She couldn't believe that's all the goddess knew. After all this time. "I'm a foundling. My family abandoned me."

"But not because they didn't want you," said Aphrodite softly. "People make choices. . . ."

"But . . . ," Pippa started.

"*You* made choices," finished Aphrodite.

Pippa clenched her fist . . . then slowly relaxed it. It was true. She had left Zeph and chosen to ride Kerauno because she loved Zeph so much. She knew it now—that's why her parents had left her. For a greater reason.

"They really loved me," she whispered.

"Yes," answered Aphrodite softly. "They did. Perhaps you or I will learn more one day. But you know the most important thing now—"

Pippa nodded. It was enough. For now.

They walked in silence, Bas still in the lead, lost in thought, too. Zeph was no longer flying but trotting along beside Pippa. Considering his earlier exertion, he was still remarkably energetic.

At length, they reached a spot where a stream gurgled, and they stopped so Zeph could take a drink. "I'm afraid I cannot go any farther with you," said Aphrodite.

"But . . . ," said Pippa, flashing the goddess a disappointed look.

Aphrodite took a deep breath. "I wish I could. But I must be present at the feast. I've caused enough trouble already." Aphrodite placed her hand gently on Pippa's shoulder. "Despite my words, I should have been there for you." From the pockets of her chiton, she drew out a bundle wrapped in cloth. "Some food for your journey. Follow the rosebushes and you will find your way. They mark a secret path, a shortcut."

"What of Ares? Will he harm my family?" Bas asked.

"I will do all I can to help you and yours," said Aphrodite. She sighed. "That god. At least there is the monsters' Pankration for him to bet on. Boxing and wrestling with the minotaur. Such contests distract him from all he's lost. More than this race, yes. He had a family once. I was going to wager with him again . . . but . . . well, I suppose we'll see. Maybe it's better to let him win one."

The goddess smiled and turned away from them, heading back up the mountain.

The three continued down the mountainside. Bas was almost skipping now, and Pippa had to hurry to keep up; Zeph trotted behind.

The goddess's reassurance about his family seemed to have lifted a weight off Bas's shoulders. Pippa still didn't know where home was, but at least she had Zeph. She was no longer alone.

She looked back lovingly at her horse. But oh no! His feathers! They were falling out, leaving a trail like snow behind him. His wings were . . . disappearing.

"Stop!" she cried, turning to face him, blocking his way. The little horse obeyed.

He seemed to notice for the first time what was happening. He glanced up the mountain, then back at Pippa. And with a happy whinny took a few more steps toward her, his feathers drifting down to the ground.

"No! Stop, Zeph!" cried Pippa. But Zeph didn't listen. He didn't seem to care. He had made his choice.

"What's happening?" Bas came running back. He saw the feathers. "Is he hurt?"

"No . . . I don't know. . . ."

Pippa touched Zeph's side, but too late—his wings were gone.

Tears filled her eyes.

"So this is what Bellerophon meant. Zeus did indeed punish you. Oh, Zeph, I'm so sorry."

But Zeph didn't seem upset. A butterfly flew by them, and he tossed his head in its direction and whinnied playfully. The butterfly landed on a rosebush, and Zeph trotted after it.

"He's all right, I think," said Bas.

Pippa wiped her eyes. "But . . . but . . ."

"You're not," continued Bas. He nudged her gently. "And that's okay too. I've been thinking. Come with me to Thessaly. Zeph too."

"Really?" Pippa asked, afraid she had misheard.

"Really. You took the blame. You convinced Zeus not to punish us. My parents will let you stay with us. I have six sisters. What's one more?"

"But surely they don't want one more mouth to feed."

"One mouth, maybe, but two hands to help. Trust me."

Pippa smiled. Trust. Just like Aphrodite had said. Bas was right; she *would* be all right. Zeph too. After all, it wasn't his wings she loved. It was him. And he was with her. He had chosen to be. Even if he couldn't fly anymore, that didn't mean their adventures were over.

She picked up a single black-tipped white feather

from the ground and slipped it into the rose brooch, just like Zeus had worn his.

Her time on Mount Olympus may have come to an end, but Pippa couldn't help feeling the real magic was just beginning.

*T*he Fates groaned and moaned. Clotho had insisted on walking rather than riding, and it was a long walk from Mount Olympus to Bas's farm in Thessaly.

When they reached the top of the hill, they leaned on their canes and peered down at the farm below. They could just see—for their old eyes were weak—a lovely white stone house with a courtyard and stables. In the pasture beyond were the horses.

One stood out from the rest. A white horse raced along with the others, faster than them all. Upon his back, two children rode, a girl and a boy, laughing and shouting and *singing the song they'd heard a year ago: "'Aloft wings beat and feathers fly, hark the horses of the sky!'"*

"See. I told you so," said Lachesis. "Love is greater than might."

Atropos sighed.

"Bother," murmured Clotho, shaking her head. "Here we go again."

But she silently thanked that mysterious force, that tangler of threads, who knew more of love and might and all such bothers, than she ever would. And then, joints creaking, she turned and joined her sisters and hobbled home.

The 25th
ΕΊΚΟΣΙ ΠΈΝΤΕ
WINGED HORSE
RACE SCROLL

Aloft wings beat and feathers fly, hark the horses of the sky!

IN MEMORY OF PEGASUS

The first winged horse of the gods and goddesses.
His power was such that everywhere on Earth
he struck his hoof, a fountain burst forth,
the most famous example being the Hippocrene spring
on Mount Helicon. But Pegasus is best known
for carrying Zeus's thunderbolts in his later years.
Because of his faithful service,
Zeus honored Pegasus by transforming him
into a constellation in the night sky
for all eternity.

Measurements
One palaiste = one hand
One pous = the length of one foot

Judge—*Zeus*

Supreme ruler of Mount Olympus,
king of the gods and goddesses,
Zeus owns the winged horse stables.

Race Officiary—*Bellerophon*

Upon Pegasus's back, Bellerophon, a mortal, fearlessly
defeated the monstrous Chimera. When Bellerophon died,
Zeus made him a demigod and assigned to him the task of
managing the winged horse stable and organizing the race.

MEET THE STEEDS OF THE 25TH RACE

Patron: *Poseidon, god of the seas*

Horse: Hali of the sea

Age and measurements: 80 years; height 20 palaiste;

wingspan 22 pous

Flag: The trident

Rider: Theodoros from Argos

Patron: Hades, god of the Underworld

Horse: Skotos, Shadow Feather

Age and measurements: 76 years; height 19.2 palaiste;

wingspan 21 pous

Flag: Cerberus

Rider: Timon, once from the island of Ithaca

Patron: Athena, goddess of wisdom

Horse: Ajax the Warrior

Age and measurements: 89 years; height 19.2 palaiste;

wingspan 22 pous

Flag: The owl

Rider: Sophia from Athens

Patron: Ares, god of war

Horse: Kerauno, Thunder Horse

Age and measurements: 78 years; height 24 palaiste;

wingspan 26 pous

Flag: The spear

Rider: Basileus from Pharsalos, in Thessaly

Patron: **Artemis, goddess of the hunt**

Horse: Argyros, Silver Wing

Age and measurements: 80 years; height 20.2 palaiste;

wingspan 22 pous

Flag: The bow

Rider: Perikles from Argos

Patron: **Hephaestus, god of metalworks**

Horse: Solon, Iron Mane

Age and measurements: 77 years; height 19 palaiste;

wingspan 21.2 pous

Flag: The ax

Rider: Dares from Boeotia

Patron: **Apollo, god of the sun**

Horse: Khruse, Fierce Brightness

Age and measurements: 76 years; height 20.2 palaiste;

wingspan 22 pous

Flag: The lyre

Rider: Khrys from Argos

Patron: **Aphrodite, goddess of love**

Horse: Zephyr of the Breeze

Age and measurements: 65 years: height 18 palaiste;

wingspan 18.2 pous

Flag: The rose

Rider: Hippolyta, presently from Athens

Patron: **Hera, goddess of marriage**

Horse: Elpis of Hope

Age and measurements: 75 years; height 20 palaiste;

wingspan 21 pous

Flag: The diadem

Rider: Leo from Elis, in Peloponnese

Patron: **Hestia, goddess of the hearth**

Horse: Eumelia the Sky Singer

Age and measurements: 82 years; height 22 palaiste;

wingspan 22.2 pous

Flag: The flame

Rider: Myron from Elis, in Peloponnese

Patron: **Demeter, goddess of grains**

Horse: Niketes, Wind's Victor

Age and measurements: 81 years; height 20.2 palaiste;

wingspan 22.2 pous

Flag: Corn

Rider: Nikos from Larissa, in Thessaly

Patron: **Dionysus, god of wine**

Horse: Meliton, Honey Wing

Age and measurements: 79 years; height 21 palaiste;

wingspan 22 pous

Flag: The goblet

Rider: Alexis from Athens

Acknowledgments

A huge thank you to all those who made this book possible, who helped in its long journey from idea to finished story. To my husband, of course. To my dad and mom, my brother and sister-in-law, and Nona and Nono (who gave me my first book of Greek myths). To the Inkslingers: Tanya Lloyd Kyi, Stacey Matson, Rachelle Delaney, Lori Sherritt, Sara Gillingham, Kay Weisman, Maryn Quarless, and Christy Goerzen. To friends Lee Edward Fodi and Vikki Vansickle. To editors Dave and Lucy and their teams, who make books happen. And to Abby, who saw its potential. To my phenomenal agent, Emily Van Beek. To the one and only Tiffany Stone, who helps me every word of the way. And to my Greek experts, Siobhan McElduff and Tom Donaghy especially, who answered my endless questions with amazing, thoughtful feedback, resources, and insights. Thank you so very, very much.